PLOUGHSHARES

Spring 1993 · Vol. 19, No. 1

GUEST EDITOR
Al Young

EXECUTIVE DIRECTOR
DeWitt Henry

MANAGING EDITOR & FICTION EDITOR
Don Lee

POETRY EDITOR
David Daniel

ASSISTANT EDITOR
Barbara Tran

FOUNDING PUBLISHER
Peter O'Malley

PLOUGHSHARES, a journal of new writing, is guest-edited serially by prominent writers, who explore different and personal visions, aesthetics, and literary circles. PLOUGHSHARES is published three times a year at Emerson College, 100 Beacon Street, Boston, MA 02116-1596. Telephone: (617) 578-8753. Phone-a-Poem: (617) 578-8754.

STAFF ASSISTANT: Barbara Lewis. ASSISTANT PROOFREADER: Holly Le-Craw Howe. POETRY READERS: Barbara Tran, Linda Russo, Tanja Brull, Tom Laughlin, Mary-Margaret Mulligan, and Jason Rogers. FICTION READERS: Billie Lydia Porter, Karen Wise, Holly LeCraw Howe, Maryanne O'Hara, Barbara Lewis, Christine Flanagan, Kimberly Reynolds, Michael Rainho, Phillip Carson, Erik Hansen, Sara Nielsen Gambrill, Tanja Brull, and David Rowell. PHONE-A-POEM COORDINATOR: Joyce Peseroff.

SUBSCRIPTIONS (ISSN 0048-4474): $19/domestic and $24/international for individuals; $22/domestic and $27/international for institutions. See last page for order form.

UPCOMING: Fall 1993, Vol. 19, Nos. 2 & 3, a fiction issue edited by Sue Miller, will appear in August 1993. Winter 1993–94, Vol. 19, No. 4, a fiction and poetry issue edited by Russell Banks and Chase Twichell, will appear in December 1993.

SUBMISSIONS: Please see back of issue for submission policies.

BACK ISSUES are available from the publisher. Write or call for abstracts and a price list. Microfilms of back issues may be obtained from University Microfilms. PLOUGHSHARES is also available as a CD-ROM full-text product from Information Access Company. INDEXED in M.L.A. Bibliography, American Humanities Index, Index of American Periodical Verse, Book Review Index. Self-index through Volume 6 available from the publisher; annual supplements appear in the fourth number of each subsequent volume.

DISTRIBUTED by Bernhard DeBoer (113 E. Centre St., Nutley, NJ 07110), Ingram Periodicals (1226 Heil Quaker Blvd., La Vergne, TN 37086), and L-S Distributors (130 East Grand Ave., South San Francisco, CA 94080). PRINTED by Edwards Brothers.

PLOUGHSHARES receives additional support from the National Endowment for the Arts, the Massachusetts Cultural Council, the Lannan Foundation, and Business Volunteers for the Arts/Boston. Major new marketing initiatives have been made possible by the Lila Wallace–Reader's Digest Literary Publishers Marketing Development Program, funded through a grant to the Council of Literary Magazines and Presses. The opinions expressed in this magazine do not necessarily reflect those of Emerson College, the editors, the staff, the trustees, or the supporting organizations.

CONTENTS

Spring 1993 · Vol. 19, No. 1

PLOUGHSHARES

Patrons

AL YOUNG

Cellar Notes: An Introduction

A gain, what's the theme?" my friend, the painter Stephen Henriques, asked. We had just enjoyed a tasty sidewalk lunch blocks from his studio in San Francisco's Richmond District. That we should be meeting to choose from his recent work a cover for this issue of *Ploughshares* seemed natural. Two books of mine—*Things Ain't What They Used to Be* and *Heaven: Collected Poems 1956–1990*—sport stunning Henriques covers. Time had ripened us both for the picking.

"*Believers*," I told him. "The theme is *Believers*. When I mentioned it over the phone to Barry Gifford—the guy who wrote *Wild at Heart*—Barry said, 'Believers in what?'"

"Oh, yes," Steve said. "Now I remember. You had to change it from something else to *Believers*, didn't you?"

"Right. Originally, the theme I'd wanted was *Celebration*. The *Ploughshares* editors told me I was going to have a hard time with that. They said they don't get many celebrative submissions."

"Why do you suppose that is?"

"It's complicated," I said. Thirty years in the lit biz, and I was mulling it over. "But some of it, I know, boils down to fashion."

While Steve and I wandered around his studio, chatting and looking at paintings, many of which had been created under the influence of music—current jazz, Latino rhythms, soloists, classic combos—portions of me couldn't help but drift.

Memory snatched me back thirty years to my coffeehouse and nightclub days, when my performing repertoire had included a brisk little ditty called "Putting on the Agony, Putting on the Style." But then I zigzagged forward to the night in the early Reagan era at a Washington, D.C., jukebox tavern, where DeWitt Henry had first approached me about guest-editing an issue. Along with writers William Fox and Beverly Lowry, we were teaching the lovely, legally blind poet Gjertrud Schnackenberg to dance. I told DeWitt I wouldn't mind doing a parody number.

Even then, I'd felt the way I feel now about life, the spirit, and imagination, all of which were slowly disappearing, it seemed, from American writing.

"I try to get with it," Trude had told us that night in D.C. "I experiment with open forms and breath lines and visual lay-outs—what everyone else is doing. But, for some reason, I always seem to end up working in iambic pentameter. I'm hopeless."

"You've found your groove," I said. "At least you aren't doing Adrienne Rich or Richard Hugo imitations. Or Ray Carver or Jayne Anne Phillips or Bobbie Ann Mason imitations. I hate what's going on in writing these days."

I still ask myself: What is it that's been strip-mining our poetry and fiction of its originality, the level of vitality that once distinguished our literature the world over? Is it the formulaic, art-by-consensus approach of creative writing workshops? Is it the rush to publish on the part of emerging writers, forced to view publication as an adjunct to advancement in a teaching career?

Besides the ubiquitous and, in basic ways, iniquitous influence of television, perhaps the bleak and flickering outlook of North American life itself has flattened and short-circuited our "imaginative" writers. After all, as a nation we have become almost robotically solipsistic and ostrich-like—to say nothing of cynical—since the Vietnam era. Would that explain the sense of sluggish withdrawal and self-entrenchment I get from cruising our main lit mags and journals? Whether cooked up or microwaved or, in any case, nuked like a standup comedy monologue, such fodder—waggishly termed McPoetry, McFiction, or McCommentary—is commonly delivered in the fragile, inorganic Styrofoam container of the present tense. But even Big Macs and Whoppers need grease, a little salt, a little onion, and some measure of "secret ingredients."

"I write the literary equivalent of a Big Mac," Stephen King once told an exacting interviewer.

Stephen King was one of the novelists my students and I wolfed down and nibbled in "Art & Trash," an oversized course I conducted at the University of California at Santa Cruz in 1989. That spring we also read and discussed Danielle Steel, Sidney Sheldon, Charles Johnson, James D. Houston, Richard Wiley, and Anne

Rice. The idea was to determine for ourselves what separated straight-ahead, best-seller storycraft and storytelling from the artful, serious kind. What put those feelie-cover paperbacks of John Updike, Toni Morrison, Scott Turow, Gore Vidal, Saul Bellow, and Alice Walker right up there on supermarket racks and airport gift shelves alongside Belva Plain, Robert Ludlum, Mary Higgins Clark, and Elmore Leonard? At the same time, Amy Tan, Terry McMillan, Rosellen Brown, Jimmy Buffett, and Ivana Trump were offstage, fixing to get in the mix.

Summarily, what the class came up with was this: There appears to have been a time when our best storytellers were also our best writers. Late in the twentieth century, however, a schism occurred: it became Creative Writing vs. Literature Lite. The nation began to produce fiction writers who were virtual pyrotechnicians and eloquent crafters of language, but who couldn't quite seem to tell a story. At the other extreme, we churned out gripping pop storytellers who often seemed oddly insensitive, neglectful, or just plain downright ignorant when it came down to questions of language or character development or thematic depth. The breakdown is simplistic, of course: many writers fall into neither camp. And students, like many of the readers they interviewed at supermarkets, actually prefer good writing *and* storytelling.

As for poetry, not many of us realize that it used to appeal to a much larger audience—collections selling far more than the two thousand copies considered respectable today. The poetry of Paul Laurence Dunbar, Edna St. Vincent Millay, Carl Sandburg, Robert Frost, Robinson Jeffers, e. e. cummings, Lawrence Ferlinghetti, and Allen Ginsberg comes to mind. Many readers whose poetry adventure or experience began with Khalil Gibran's *The Prophet* or with Rod McKuen's *Stanyan Street & Other Sorrows* moved on to "heavier" or headier stuff.

And, don't forget, had it not been for the nearly 100,000 copies sold of *Fruits & Vegetables,* her maiden poetry collection, Erica Jong may not have gotten that contract with Holt for her smash novel *Fear of Flying.* As a Holt author myself at the time, publishing novels and books of poetry, *I* haven't forgotten. Nor have I forgotten how Nikki Giovanni—America's most widely known and translated poet in the early 1980s—kicked off her career and moved 80,000 copies of her first book by hawking a broadside for one dollar apiece at readings. Poet Dana Gioia's invaluable analysis of the poetry scene, which prompted his eloquent call for the deprivatization of poetry ("Can Poetry Matter?," *The Atlantic,* May 1991) remains accurate and resonant.

During a 1990 lecture and reading tour of Bangladesh and India, sponsored by the U.S. Information Agency's Arts America Program, I thought a great deal about Mr. Gioia's observations and prescriptive comments. During the question-and-answer segment that followed my talks throughout the subcontinent—Dhaka, Bombay, Bhopal, Madras, Bangalore, New Delhi, and in the countryside and remote provinces—high school and university students and their teachers and professors routinely inquired, "What's going on in your country, Mr. Young? The only stories and poems we read that tell us anything about everyday life in the United States come from the blacks, the Latinos, the Asian Americans . . . Others, the whites, the majority—whatever they are called now—their writing often seems so disconnected from the country's problems we read about. Why are American writers so coded, so . . . so private?"

Inevitably, I dealt with this question by pointing out that culture is the most valuable product any society produces. In South Asia, this truth required no explanation or embellishment. And, since Bangladeshis and Indians understand that art is thoroughly reflective of a given culture, it was easy to remind those attending my presentations that the short stories one reads in *The New Yorker,* in annuals, and in literary journals do indeed mirror the consciousness of a segment of America that has, in fact, disconnected itself. Not only do many of the poets and writers in the U.S. take no interest in what's going on in the rest of the world, many truly neither know nor notice what's going on in their own country. Psychologically, it sometimes feels as though we've suffered excessively from the corporate dismemberment of awareness and its deep-freezing of consciousness.

"There was even a time," I told an audience in Bhopal, where thousands had died or sustained serious injuries in a Union Carbide industrial accident, "when our fiction and poetry were overrun with brand names such as K-Mart and Gucci and Sony. We Americans tend to identify ourselves with brand-name products and the images they project. So much so, that people who drive a BMW or a Mercedes-Benz automobile actually think they're superior to anyone who drives a less expensive car, or takes the bus or the subway, or walks.

"This goes on in the art world, too. Many novice poets and fiction writers think it's important to plug into a going style or sound. And this is fine, while you're still learning your art, your craft—the tricks and all. But the late Seventies and Eighties seem to have killed off the idea of originality, as well as the idea of mastering something classic. More than ever in American life now, focus is on the so-called individual and on individual personality. Once writers grow rich or famous, they're imitated."

Toward the close of 1992, while I was winding up a teaching visit at the University of Michigan, Ann Arbor, and poring over the scores of *Ploughshares* submissions posted batch by batch from Boston, Knopf brought out an intriguing new book called *The Art of Celebration: 20th Century Painting, Literature, Sculpture, Photography, and Jazz.* Written by Alfred Appel, Jr., Professor of English and American culture at Northwestern, this exuberant testament to the health and well-being of the celebrative urge in modern art prompted, to my surprise, a full-page review in *The New York Times Book Review.* "To be as unabashedly enthusiastic as Mr. Appel takes courage," wrote art scholar Nicholas Fox Wever. "But he is determined in his goal of shattering the 'tired half-truth' that modernism is 'unfathomably abstract and obscure.' He treats as the enemy 'the newest academic fog banks' that obscure the more joyous, life-embracing sides of recent art. Instead, he explores the ways that certain artistic achievements of this century represent connection more than severance—their links to archaic sources and to myriad exciting aspects of everyday life."

Writers, painters, sculptors, photographers, filmmakers, and jazz musicians, by the jetload, are pouring out of college and university Masters of Fine Arts programs, where I myself sometimes teach. Cheek by jowl with literary scholars and theorists, musicologists, art historians, and aestheticians, these artists-to-be are studying their craft. I theorize that this late twentieth-century development might explain why yea-saying exuberance and heart-on-sleeve inventiveness have become so hard to locate. I mean the kinds of life-endorsing oomph and zest that make art in all its forms so inconceivably affecting—from those undatable, unbeatable cave paintings at Altamira and Lascaux, to the head of Nefertiti, Chaucer, Li Po, and Noh plays, to kachina dolls, Mozart, tango, cakewalk, Georgia O'Keeffe, Sergei Eisenstein, and the room-moving, soul-bracing sound of Dexter Gordon's tenor saxophone.

That's why I was so pleased to discover, after I'd picked the poems and stories for this issue, that all the work had something in common: reverence; passionate beliefs and loves.

I tried to explain as much to Stephen Henriques in his studio, where an LP recording of youthful Cuban jazz pianist Gonzalo Rubalcaba was spinning on a new Roksan super-turntable, weaving fresh, beguiling webs of sound that rose and swayed and quivered, then hovered. "You can check it out for yourself," I told Steve. "Writers were putting across something they either believed *in,* or *believed*! And I love that. Passion, emotion, and sentiment are pretty much considered passé nowadays. One poet even apologized in advance for the passion in one of the poems she submitted; she knew most editors would disapprove."

"Amazing," said Steve. "And it's funny, too. That's what I'm all about—passion and feeling. And color and rhythm."

At that, we stopped and zeroed in on the music. The astonishing Gonzalo Rubalcaba, whom Dizzy Gillespie had encouraged during visits to Cuba, was thrilling us with his take on John Coltrane's "Giant Steps."

"Well," I said, "you remember what Lester Young said about that?"

"About what?"

" 'Invention is a mother!' That's what Prez said."

Steve got to his feet. "Oh, man," he sighed, "you don't have to remind me. I listen to this stuff and start painting to it, trying to capture what I'm hearing and feeling and remembering and seeing. It's funny, when I started painting full time, I had to learn how to paint all over again."

"How do you mean?"

"You know how it is. You paint your way through art school, then you have to learn to unpaint."

I reached for my camera; it was snapshot time. I wanted to get some pictures of Stephen Henriques's studio just as it was, before the afternoon had reached the last of its groove, and time flipped over into twilight.

"Hey," Steve yelled from another room, "take all the pictures you want. I'll get the slides I've already made of this new stuff. But be thinking about what you want for a cover."

Believers, I thought one more time, then clicked and flashed my way around the room.

L. E. SCOTT

Synapse and Grace

In heaven there is no beer. That's why:

There was a bar outside of Pigeon Forge, crawled back onto a flat space hanging off its mountain, where someone, seemingly inspired by great forces, had seen the fiction of her body, and in tribute rendered it fantastically, overwhelmingly, in fluorescent paints across the entirety of the back wall. The unregistered image of Dolly's hair, Dolly's breasts, Dolly's hips, and Dolly's lavender, blood-tight jumpsuit was depicted in glorious, drowning sexism, making what seemed to be an almost patriotic appeal to the tongue and eyes, a body enthusiasm so palpable that upon seeing the painting and recognizing its subject for what she was, Brian felt physically slowed by it. He stopped in the doorway and clutched himself with his invisible arms. He sensed that the painting was hungry for northern flesh.

He chose his seat carefully, assuming a stool at the bar which put him in direct confrontation with the mammoth ideal of Dolly's hips, and the brush-stroked lines of her crotch intersected in such a way that his eyes were quite naturally led to the display of top-shelf liquors—this way to the Chivas, almost. This quirk of composition may have been purposeful genius on the part of the artist, but considering the work as a whole, Brian suspected it was not. It was impossible to see the entire painting properly in such cramped quarters, as she had been painted, or applied, directly on the back boards with all the intent and majesty of a tobacco advertisement on the side of a barn. The bar itself was too close-walled and elongated, like a generous, ill-lit corridor, and Brian had the brief sensation of being a passenger on a ship in a bottle.

And yet this was not his first encounter with the work of visionaries. At least not since he had left his home and his wife, that first life, behind. After all, he had seen the temple through the trees: the palace in West Virginia, Krishna gold. A shimmering dome, visible from the icy interstate.

No, that wasn't true. It couldn't be. No kind of preacher would have his temple in all of that gray. Bhahatapur...Bhatapapa...what was that guy's name? He was supposed to be some kind of really big deal, a Krishna Pope or something. Better, a Krishna Joseph Smith. Brian had seen his photo in a magazine article and was struck by the exotically musical name attributed to this mundane-looking bald guy with glasses. With glasses, of all things. The sign must have spelled it out, must have, and he could almost see it—Bhapapa...no. And now he remembered that sign, quite clearly. It was a billboard sneaking up along with others as he'd rounded the curves of the overpass. Not the real thing at all.

And that fake preacher with the Sears economy glasses—he had an awful lot of things that shouldn't be his, didn't he? A golden house, and all those women. Very *unusual* women, at that. What a strange life. It wasn't that Brian envied him exactly, but still. He had that beautiful name.

Brian wished he could remember what it was. He wondered what perfect syllables he'd string together if he were the one who got wrapped in sheets and had to choose a new name for himself. It was so clear now, he felt embarrassed. The sign, with its cartoon-painted dome, existed in the same stinking, airy field as other, less ridiculous images: radio call letters, news personalities, cigarette boxes, and giant women dressed in black velvet. It was almost like television, like the driving and the seeing were no more real than a long, boring, made-for-TV movie.

Things were slipping, melting together. Before he'd left, Madeline, his wife, had pronounced him dead, said he was "cracking up." Cracking, strange word. The billboard over Huntington, he'd at least seen that. Proof positive that even if there weren't worlds within worlds, there were, at least, worlds *behind* worlds. It was the kind of evidence that would set him off, make him over-think, causing a little ghost to churn up heat in his upper chest where he'd once had an ulcer in his esophagus.

The Krishnas had advertised their heaven like a theme park or a Stuckey's. And maybe he'd really seen what they meant. Maybe he did see a temple, but he'd thought it was real. Gold, and then the green, and then the gray clouds, and then pure white smoke coming up from the industrial chimneys over Huntington, enveloping Hatfields and McCoys and Hare Krishna Babbadab-ba...almost heaven. Was that it?

The television was on, down by Dolly's head. Brian could make out that it was a James Bond movie, but he didn't remember which. The villain was a black guy with a hook for a hand or something, and he was throwing a plate of pale meat into a pond, to which alligators responded appropriately. The muscles in Brian's shoulders began to tighten, reacting to a nonexistent cold wind. He wanted to contain this habit of nursing his own sensual distortions. To calm himself, Brian sought the predictability of the veneer-topped bar; he traced the wood-grain patterns, his rigid fingertip acting as an agent of total concentration.

Because Dolly was in a relaxed, lounging pose, on her side, her hair punched into an oceanic swell by her own enormous hand, one end of the bar was more crowded than the other. Regulars, Brian figured, privileged seating. It was tough to get served down where he was. The yellow light from the hot dog case cast mostly up, on the Breasts, but the arm's length of cleavage appeared blue. For a moment, the bartender's head was turned just right, and was haloed by Dolly's top nipple.

Brian heard music, barely. A woman moaning from a dislo-cated radio. He wondered if it was her, but he would not linger on the possibility. He couldn't afford to be so associational. "I need a draft down here. Anything." He was noticed at last. "And a hot dog. Plain." The bartender moved to serve him, but Brian could only sense that from his peripheral vision, as he couldn't prevent his gaze from straying toward the splendor of the Dolly.

"Plain?" repeated the bartender.

"Yeah—um, I mean yes, thank you." Brian knew he should try to sound less distracted, be cool, but he couldn't help himself. His mind, such as it was, swirled. His eyes sort of ached from the expanse, the work of taking it all in. "Wow," he said, and he heard himself sounding very boyish. Brian was thirty-seven. "That's very impressive," and his voice climbed even higher.

The bartender responded with a strange, appreciative smile and just enough hesitant shuffling to let Brian know that he was ordering his lunch from none other than the artist himself.

"Ahh!" squeaked Brian, "then you—" He pointed at the wall. There was tension in his throat, a mechanical failure, and he couldn't tell what it was from. It was very frustrating. He wished he could get his beer, already. Maybe it would help to relax his voice. His finger was still out in the air, and the bartender was smiling broadly. Then he stepped aside in a way that was both prideful and self-mocking.

"Uh-hmm," he confirmed. And Brian nearly forgot his own partial question. "Jesus," said Brian, with what he hoped was a positive-sounding reverence and a manly sounding depth. He felt as though his body were barely containing three inconvenient, conflicting animals: one mesmerized by the physical pull of the painting, one trying to express a newly adolescent vocalization, and one trying to order lunch. Cracking. Brian really wanted that beer, but the bartender was still keen on discussing his handi-work with this northern critic.

"I could have put a mirror back there. A lot of places, you'll see a mirror behind the bar. I don't know about that, myself. Not my taste."

Brian nodded.

"I mean, who the hell would want to watch hisself drinking a beer or chewing his food or smoking"—the bartender moved his rag-swathed hand in a series of small loops to indicate the small cycles of choice—"when he could look at her instead?" The bartender turned his attention toward the television momentarily and missed Brian's respectful shrug. Brian compensated with an agreeing grunt.

Brian ventured, perhaps too carefully, "She is an achievement. I must ask you—" and then he couldn't find the words. Stumbling, he tried again, "Rather, I would say, the most amazing aspect seems—"

The bartender squinted at Brian and asked, " 'Scuse me?"

"I'm sorry. I was just wondering how daunting a task it was to, say... map out the particulars." Brian realized that he was making a sort of flipping gesture with his left hand, as he spoke, snapping it around from the wrist, palm out but close to the chest. He suspected that it appeared fey, so he dropped his hands to his lap self-consciously.

"I don't think I get you. You from up north?"

"Yeah." Brian was beginning to feel embarrassed. "I guess I mean the proportions. She's so, well, expansive. And close."

The bartender smiled. "Yes sir, that's my favorite part. My boy and me drew her out in pencil first, going by a magazine picture. Took half a day to get it right."

"Prodigious. Quite."

"Then we filled her in. You a schoolteacher?" asked the bartender, and he turned his back to Brian, then adding, possibly, but it was too mumbled to tell for sure, "or just an asshole?"

Brian was a little shocked. Quietly, he confirmed, "I used to take children's photos at K-Mart, but on occasion I've taught. Photography for an Adult Ed program. Back in Ohio."

"So you're a real artist, huh? Cincinnati?"

Brian wanted to ask the man if he was making fun of him, but he was intimidated by the breadth of the bartender's sweat-stained, white shirt back and the prominence of his powerfully grinding shoulder blades. With an inaudible sigh, Brian answered, "Been there. But no. I'm from Akron."

The bartender's back said, "Pabst?"

"No. No catsup. Plain."

"Huh?"

"Hmm?"

"*Draft. Pabst.*"

"*Please.*"

Brian's face warmed uncomfortably. He looked down at his hands and noticed that they looked thinner and weaker in the diffused illumination of beer signs and the portion of slight sun allowed through small block windows. Perhaps the "cracking" notion was doubly true. What Madeline meant was that he was losing his mind, that she had noticed a change in him, a steady creeping toward conservatism which she had assumed was politically charged, and so she'd refused to take it seriously, at first. But he'd succeeded in unnerving her with his increased tendency toward stillness.

He'd embraced immotility as one might embrace a new religion. It was not just a technique for control, but it was *in* him—a brewing, un-bibled philosophy and just as volatile. His mood was such a fragile one, too easily disrupted. She couldn't vacuum when he was home, or he'd become agitated and suspicious, like his mother's old dachshund. Deep colors and new sounds tended to make him anxious. So did the perfumes of their house, or the disparities of light from room to room. She would find him sometimes, in the frame of a paralyzing doorway, his jaw set against some unexpressed desire. Or he'd be incomprehensible in his talk, make her cry by telling her outright that her "abstractions were sinister," and he would accuse her of pretending not to understand him.

In retrospect, Brian reasoned that Madeline's "cracking" accusation was too mild, obviously tempered by her affection. She should have been more specific, more cruel to him. As it was, the combination of their intimacy and her kindness had proved unbearable. He'd hit the road after shattering a jar of spaghetti sauce on the kitchen floor, having found himself incapable of cleaning it up. He'd watched her on the floor, with her paper towels, dustpan, and an unwieldy broom, moving rhythmically, without tiredness, while he stood disabled on just one square foot of linoleum tile. Pleasure, terror, and impotence all inhabited the very same breath. That last image was of her rump, high in the air, and she'd steadied herself on two knees and an elbow, not knowing that an escaped strand of her dark hair was trailing in the spilt sauce. And he couldn't tell her about it.

The other sense of cracking was his own private one; the physical crack at the base of his skull, invisible cleft, a schism of flesh he felt spreading at night when he lay his head into the pillow, an activity which had recently developed into a ceremony: the lowering of the head, the placing of the brain—the ritual of sinking encased plutonium to the bottom of the sea. Preventing him from sleep, he'd sense splitting under the cerebellum, he'd sense a leaking crack in the barrel. Madeline had whined for him to see a doctor. She thought he had arthritis, or some other bone-stiffening disease.

Brian swiveled on his stool, pretending to be bored, careful not to make uncool eye contact with any of the other patrons. The wall behind him was patchworked with neon beer signs and posters of unknown women cuddling frosty bottles between their legs and breasts.

They seemed so ordinary. Not one of them capable of sparking the near-religious creativity that Dolly had. They were too human, too vulnerable to abuse. Miniature glories at best. Why didn't they just wilt or mildew or disintegrate, having to face the great wall of Dolly?

He was steadily losing the memory of his wife's sad face, but with what impression of her was left, he tried to compare against the sexually worked expressions of the women from the posters. There was a difference, sure, but not one that could be so easily expressed as, "Well, she is wanting, and Madeline does not," or "These lips seem so much softer, wetter..." Rather, the difference was a matter of bones and a lack of stillness and something to do with the very separate mind of the body which caused Madeline to appear to be in constant movement, in constant process.

That appearance, his awareness of Madeline's process, caused his cells to crawl. He got hot flashes, spots on his scalp and cheek that would burn if he made too many connections in his musings. It was the familiar anxiety he couldn't shake, inexplicably the same sense of dread he'd suffered when he, as a boy, had watched other boys trap panicked creatures in their hands—mice or lizards. They seemed to do it just for the strange pleasure of observing tiny hearts beating hard under the skin of delicate bodies. As a witness, his willingness and repulsion were irreconcilable.

Brian began to formulate a theory of proportional relationships between the level of his excitements and his sense of potential energy in other bodies. Particularly female ones, which he subcategorized as escaping, trapped, and static. If Madeline's unyielding vitality represented one extreme of this continuum of stimulating objects, then Dolly, in her treasured fix, constituted... Brian hadn't noticed before that there were some slight imperfections in the surface of the painting, especially where there was a greater thickness of paint, as in the great curving swell of Dolly's lavender hip. Small fissures, of the kind which plagued Da Vinci's work, appeared as nerve patterns, disrupting the illusion of Dolly's immutable nature. It was obvious an attempt had been made toward maintenance; new paint had been applied to touch up the gaps of the old, but the fractures still left shadows for the studious to detect. Brian quelled an urge to point out that he was not the only one who was cracking. A sudden rush of warmth made his fingertips feel like they were about to burst.

New music came stronger from the radio. Stations were being changed by an unseen hand. Roused from his fantasy, Brian looked around, embarrassed, but no one knew what he was thinking. No eye singled him out and saw through. No eye desired to. He counted in his head, steadied himself. He pretended that there was a way to order noise and light, a way to cope with all the stimuli.

The food and beer came. "That's two eighty-five," said the bartender, "and that's no joke." Tight in the face, Brian paid up, clumsily counting out the tip. He noticed that Bond's situation had changed for the worse. The superagent was running across alligators' backs, and their jaws were snapping in time with his steps. Wild. It looked nice and warm there where the alligators were. Florida. Brian drained his beer and ordered another. Those conflicting animals were settling down to slumber, but slowly. Dolly's lines were softer, more lovely, than when he had first come in to this place. She wasn't so hard to look at, after all. There was an ultimate, permanent stillness in the way she lay, as fixed as a gigantic Vargas girl.

"Pabst," he mouthed, out of respect for the language they spoke down here.

Dolly. Even her faults were in an arrested state. She was, above all things, reliable. It would be possible to return to her again and again and detect no process, no tainting movement, save the natural progress of entropy. Hers was the true vocation of an idol, or a loved one. Goddesses, unlike women, were traditionally wrought from singular materials: bronze, stone, and paint. So function knew no trouble in matching the form. Deep comfort was settling in Brian, as deep as liquor, as deep as statuary. Her mouth was non-potential, her body, completely achieved. He felt inspired to discreetly cross himself in her lavender presence and silently ask for an ungrantable forgiveness. Her lack of response was what he'd sought, was what was given. I suspect reverie, he confessed, and was not blessed by her.

The bar was filling up with men who had just finished work for the day, and Brian rose against that tide of seekers as he walked toward the door. He made eye contact with a few of them, pretending he was recognizable in these parts. The day's-end smell of bodies came in from the frequently opened doorway, borne on cold, snowless air, which Brian savored. Descending the mountain at night would be easy, he thought, because he'd never know how close the car was to falling over an edge. He glanced at the television just before he left:

Bond in the arms of an incredibly beautiful woman. Very warm in Florida. Jane Seymour.

Jane Seymour.

New Vrindaban.

Bhaktipada.

Some things just click. Renewed and impervious, he wasn't startled by the door slamming back on its springs behind him. He was distracted by the notion of taking detours through wealthier neighborhoods to explore their fancy graveyards; he thought he might visit some granite angels.

Coyote Seduces a Statue

One glimpse—that's all,
   then in no time flat,
Coyote's beguiled,
   spit-shine kempt:
cologne-scented singer,
   bouquet-bringer, acrobatic
twister into arabesques:
   What can I change?
What's the sure-fire ingredient?
   How many howls
make a billet-doux?
   Good luck, sings the swan-white moon,
good luck and let me know—

   No desert crones,
no love-is-cowbones
   cynics can quell
his in-a-hurry heart:
   he wants the polestar
as a wedding preacher,
   a cactus for the breakneck
matrimony's witness,
   brisk Rabbit to give the bride away—

Have you ever felt
   your plumed-chapeau strategy,
your happy-ever-aftering hid
   a dunce-cap desire?
Tell me now.
   Have you ever found
a glowing storefront rose
   at closer range

to be the flimsiest, most gimcrack
    counterfeit?
Surely once or twice.
    Have you ever felt your jukebox nights
collapsing—nod your head if you have—
    into migraine dawns,
like the black pulse of dominoes
    dropping to earth?—

On a hot hill's pedestal,
    on a sky-high hill,
what the snatch-gossip birds,
    the yolk-bright sun reveal:
the stock-still, not-murmuring lips,
    the stiff, ungenial arms:
Coyote has seduced a statue!

Our Star

Every day, whether we realize it or not,
we choose one of two stars to guide us,
a star as ephemeral as our life,
a star water can wash away. One star
is made of packed sugar, the other
of packed salt. Water melts both.
If we choose the star of sugar
we will follow all the sweet things
of the earth, the candied surfaces
that glisten, reflecting a honeyed light.
If salt, we will go the way of the seas—
restless, tossing broken dolls
and the timbers of drowned ships
onto everyone's shore.

            The way of salt
is the way of sorrow and loss,
for salt seeds every tear
before it blossoms, just as death
seeds every birth. Salt is the pillar
erected to those who have looked
when they were warned not to.

At night the star illuminates our sleep,
yet before dawn it is washed away,
so that each morning we must choose again.
The poor choose the star of salt.
They break it into pieces, grind it up,
and eat it with their rough bread.
Salt is the only star in their heaven.
It is no choice at all. Invariably
the rich choose the star of sugar.

Under its light they build roads
that pass the shanties of the poor
and lead to gingerbread mansions.

I choose the star of salt. I follow it
into grocery stores and factories.
The cashiers and barbers watch me,
and the steelworkers and foreign pickers
bent over shovels or rows of lettuce.
They are silent, brooding, distrustful.
Each morning I choose their star
because it is my star also,
because it is the rich man's star,
although he doesn't know it, not yet.
Every morning I choose this star
because the salt grains hiss
on the shore as the sea washes up
the ground bones of the starless dead.

My Aloneness

Nights standing in a field
or sleeping under the stars,
I sense that one of those pebbles
of light must be signaling me
from deep space. I know
this is no more than my own
longing cast like fishing line
into the depths of another
kind of ocean, and that
my aloneness is reflected
in whatever rock chip
I can imagine out there,
but there's a comfort I
won't deny in the images
and word groupings I invent,
no matter how outlandish
or ornate they are, or bare.
And when I realize
that nothing is going
to respond to my bait,
and I'm standing at the edge
of a bustling milky stream
packed with sparkling shards
of dumb rock, there's something
terrifying yet wonderful
about acknowledging
my complete aloneness that only
this procedure can impart,
like standing one foggy dawn

ankle-deep in a freezing brook
with no one else around
just as the sun burns through
and the trees like tattered thoughts
release the hidden circle of the sky—
endless, empty, cold, and blue.

CARL PHILLIPS

What Myth Is

Not only what lasts, but what
applies over time also. So
maybe, for all my believing, not

you, on either count. Any more
than this hand where it falls,
here, on your body; or than

your body itself, however good
sometimes at making—even now,
in sleep—a point carry. Not

this morning, either, that under
the heat has already begun
failing; nor, for all their pre–

Ice Age glamour—what is
mythical, at best, not myth—
these Japanese beetles that off

and on hit the window's limp
screen, fall in, even. Who
make of the trees' leaves a

thin lace the air, like memory,
languidly fingers. Whose wings,
like yours where sometimes I

see them, flash broad, green-
gold in the sun, to say bronze.
When they fold them, it's hard

to believe they fly, ever.

Michigan August

Far from Puebla and Michoacán
men wake to pick
peaches and beans.
Light rolls out its bolt of cloth.
Yard sales, craft shows, the six-pack
loneliness of rural towns.
On either side of I-95, going to Sonora,
butterflies don't care
who drives more than fifty-five
for a cheap pint of faith
in the jackpots.
Mars Bars and Milky Ways
at the Seven-Eleven. Shots of Diana Ross,
Madonna, home-grown Michigan stars,
plastered on thin-walled rooms
sirens fill with blue police
in a dream.

Seasonal

This time each year nothing stirs.
The slow earth clings
to its few known elements.

Its moon lights only this tenth
of the century. Autumn's madness
has left the trees. Winter's sad mists, too.

Between seasons, always waiting
on the window's other side, irregular
shadows filter the already fine winds
in which a stranger might appear
before a womanly shape could claim her.

The Day the Leaves Came

For so long the hillside shone white,
the white of white branches laden, the sky
more white, the river unmoved.

And when the first stirrings started
underneath, the hollowing subtle,
unpredictable, rotten crust gave way—

ice water up to the ankle! She
turned from her work and shook
her wet foot. The buds had broken.

Not the green of birches in full leaf.
Not meadow, tundra, berry patch, tussock.
For this moment only, this green—

the touch of one loved
in secret, a gasp held in,
let go.

Censored

Because we suspect
ourselves, knowing
what we're capable of, knowing

how thin the veneer,
wanting to control
what gets away from us

even now, with restraints
wrists, ankles,
our chastity belted down

so we can save ourselves
for and from. Because in our visions
our best moments

we all speak forbidden
languages. Because if anyone
knew us, really,

they could not
love us. This goes
for God, triple.

CAROLYN FERRELL

Proper Library

Boys, men, girls, children, mothers, babies. You got to feed them. You always got to keep them fed. Winter summer. They always have to feel satisfied. Winter summer. But then you stop and ask: Where is the food going to come from? Because it's never-ending, never-stopping. Where? Because your life is spent on feeding them and you never stop thinking about where the food is going to come from.

Formula, pancakes, syrup, milk, roast turkey with cornbread stuffing, Popsicles, love, candy, tongue kisses, hugs, kisses behind backs, hands on faces, warmth, tenderness, Boston cream pie, fucking in the butt. You got to feed them, and it's always going to be you. Winter summer.

My ma says to me, Let's practice the words this afternoon when you get home, baby. I nod to her. I don't have to use any words with her to let her know I will do what she wants. When family people come over and they see me and Ma in the kitchen like that with the words, they say she has the same face as the maid in the movies. She does have big brown hands like careful shovels, and she loves to touch and pat and warm you up with them. And when she walks, she shuffles. But if anyone is like the maid in the movies, it is Aunt Estine. She likes to give mouth, 'specially when I got the kids on my hands. She's sassy. She's got what people call a bad attitude. She makes sure you hear her heels clicking all the time, 'specially when you are lying in bed before dawn and thinking things in order, how you got to keep moving, all day long. Click, click. Ain't nobody up yet? Click. Lazy-ass Negroes, you better not be 'specting me to cook y'all breakfast when you do get up! Click, click. I'm hungry. Click. I don't care what time it is, I'm hungry y'all and I'm tired and depressed and I need someone to talk to. Well, the hell with all y'all. That's my last word. Click, click, click.

My ma pats her hands on my schoolbag, which is red like a girl's, but that's all right. She pats it like it was my head. The books I have in it are: Biology, Woodworking for You, Math 1, The History of Civilization.

I'm supposed to be in Math 4, but the people keep holding me back. I know it's no real fault of mine. I been teaching the kids Math 4 from a book I took out the Lending Mobile in the schoolyard. The kids can do most of Math 4. They like the way I teach it to them, with real live explanations, not the kind where you are supposed to have everything already in your head and it's just waiting to come out. And the kids don't ask to see if I get every one right. They trust me. They trust my smart. They just like the feel of the numbers and seeing them on a piece of paper: division of decimals, division of fractions. It's these numbers that keep them moving and that will keep them moving when I am gone. At school I just keep failing the City Wide Tests every May and the people don't ask any questions: they just hold me back. Cousin Cee Cee said, If you wasn't so stupid you would realize the fact of them holding you back till you is normal.

The kids are almost as sad as Ma when I get ready to go to school in the morning. They cry and whine and carry on and ask me if they can sit on my lap just one more time before I go, but Ma is determined. She checks the outside of my books to make sure nothing is spilled over them or that none of the kids have torn out any pages. Things got to be in place. There got to be order if you gonna keep on moving, and Ma knows that deep down. This morning I promise to braid Lasheema's hair right quick before I go, and as I'm braiding, she's steady smiling her four-year-old grin at Shawn, who is a boy and therefore has short hair, almost a clean shave, and who can't be braided and who weeps with every strand I grease, spread, and plait.

Ma warns me, Don't let them boys bother you now, Lorrie. Don't let 'em.

I tell her, Ma, I have not let you down in a long time. I know what I got to do for you.

She smiles but I know it is a fake smile, and she says, Lorrie, you are my only son, the only real man I got. I don't want them boys to get you from me.

I tell her because it's the only thing I can tell her, You cooking up something special tonight?

Ma smiles and goes back to fixing pancake mix from her chair in the kitchen. The kids are on their way to forgetting about me 'cause they love pancakes more than anything and that is the only way I'll get out of here today. Sheniqua already has the bottle of Sugar Shack Syrup and Tonya is holding her plate above her nappy lint head.

Tommy, Lula Jean's Navy husband, meets me at the front door as I open it. Normally he cheers me up by testing me on Math 4 and telling me what a hidden genius I am, a still river running deep, he called it one time. He likes to tell me jokes and read stories from the Bible out loud. And he normally kisses my sister Lula Jean right where I and everybody else can see them, like in the kitchen or in the bedroom on the bed, surrounded by at least nine kids and me, all flaming brown heads and eyes. He always says: This is what love should be. And he searches into Lula Jean's face for whole minutes.

I'm leaving for Jane Addams High School and I meet Tommy and he has a lady tucked under his arm and it ain't Lula Jean. Her hair is wet and smells like mouthwash and I hate him in a flash. I never hate anybody, but now I hate him. I know that when I close the door behind me a wave of mouths will knock Tommy and this new lady down but it won't drown them. My sister Anita walks into the room and notices and carries them off into the bathroom, quick and silent. But before that she kisses me on my cheek and pats her hand, a small one of Ma's, on my chest. She whispers, You are my best man, remember that. She slips a letter knife in my jacket pocket. She says, If that boy puts his thing on you, cut it off. I love you, baby. She pushes me out the door.

Layla Jackson who lives in the downtown Projects and who might have AIDS comes running up to me as I walk out our building's door to the bus stop. She is out of breath. I look at her and could imagine a boy watching her chest heave up and down like that and suddenly get romantic feelings, it being so big and all, split like two kickballs bouncing. I turn my eyes to hers, which are crying. Layla Jackson's eyes are red. She has her baby Tee Tee in her arms but it's cold out here and she doesn't have a blanket on him or nothing. I say to her, Layla, honey, you gonna freeze that baby to death.

And I take my jacket off and put it over him, the tiny bundle.

Layla Jackson says, Thanks Lorrie man I got a favor to ask you please don't tell me no please man.

Layla always makes her words into a worry sandwich.

She says, Man, I need me a new baby-sitter 'cause I been took Tee Tee over to my mother's but now she don't want him with the others and now I can't do nothing till I get me a sitter.

I tell her, Layla, I'm going back to school now. I can't watch Tee Tee in the morning but if you leave him with me in the cafeteria after fifth period I'll take him on home with me.

She says, That means I got to take this brat to Introduction to Humanities with me. Shit, man. He's gonna cry and I won't pass the test on Spanish Discoverers. Shit, man.

Then Layla Jackson thinks a minute and says, Okay, Lorrie, I'll give Tee to you at lunch in the cafeteria, bet. And I'll be 'round your place 'round six for him or maybe seven, thanks, man.

Then she bends down and kisses Tee Tee on his forehead and he glows with what I know is drinking up an oasis when you are in the desert for so long. And she turns and walks to the downtown subway, waving at me. At the corner she comes running back because she still has my jacket and Tee Tee is waving the letter knife around like a flag. She says that her cousin Rakeem was looking for me and to let me know he would waiting for me 'round his way. *Yes.* I say to her, See you, Layla, honey.

Before I used to not go to Jane Addams when I was supposed to. I got in the habit of looking for Rakeem, Layla's cousin, underneath the Bruckner Expressway, where the Spanish women sometimes go to buy oranges and watermelons and apples cheap. He was what you would call a magnet, only I didn't know that then. I didn't understand the different flavors of the pie. I saw him one day and I had a feeling like I wanted him to sit on my lap and cradle me. That's when I had to leave school. Rakeem, he didn't stop me. His voice was just as loud as the trucks heading towards Manhattan on the Bruckner above us: This is where your real world begins, man. The women didn't watch us. We stared each other in the eyes. Rakeem taught me how to be afraid of school and of people watching us. He said, Don't go back, and I didn't. A part of me was saying that his ear was more delicious than Math 4. I didn't go to Jane Addams for six months.

On the BX 17 bus I see Tammy Ferguson and her twins and Joe Smalls and that white girl Laura. She is the only white girl in these Bronx projects that I know of. I feel sorry for her. She has blue eyes and red hair and one time when the B-Crew-Girls were going to beat her butt in front of the building, she broke down crying and told them that her real parents were black from the South. She told them she was really a Negro and they all laughed and that story worked the opposite than we all thought. Laura became their friend, like the B-Crew-Girls' mascot. And now she's still their friend. People may laugh when she ain't around but she's got her back covered. She's loyal and is trying to wear her thin flippy hair in cornrows, which in the old days woulda made the B-Crew, both boys and girls, simply fall out. When Laura's around, the B-Crew-Girls love to laugh. She looks in my direction when I get on the bus and says, Faggot.

She says it loud enough for all the grown-up passengers to hear. They don't look at me, they keep their eyes on whatever their eyes are on, but I know their ears are on me. Tammy Ferguson always swears she would never help a white girl, but now she can't pass up this opportunity, so she says, You tight-ass homo, go suck some faggot dick. Tammy's kids are taking turns making hand-prints on the bus window.

I keep moving. It's the way I learned: keep moving. I go and sit next to Joe Smalls in the back of the bus and he shows me the Math 3 homework he got his baby's mother Tareen to do for him. He claims she is smarter now than when she was in school at Jane Addams in the spring. He laughs.

The bus keeps moving. I keep moving even though I am sitting still. I feel all of the ears on us, on me and Joe and the story of Tareen staying up till 4 a.m. on the multiplication of fractions and then remembering that she had promised Joe some ass earlier but seeing that he was sound asleep snoring anyway, she worked on ahead and got to the percent problems by the time the alarm went off. Ha ha. Joe laughs, I got my girl in deep check. Ha ha.

All ears are on us, but mainly on me. Tammy Ferguson is busy slapping the twins to keep quiet and sit still, but I can feel Laura's eyes like they are a silent machine gun. Faggot faggot suck dick faggot. Now repeat that one hundred times in one minute and that's how I am feeling.

Keep moving. The bus keeps rolling and you also have to keep moving. Like water like air like outer space. I always pick something for my mind. Like today I am remembering the kids and how they will be waiting for me after fifth period and I remember the feel of Lasheema's soft dark hair.

Soft like the dark hair that covers me, not an afro, but silky hair, covering me all over. Because I am so cold. Because I am so alone. A mat of thick delicious hair that blankets me in warmth. And therefore safety. And peace. And solitude. And ecstasy. Lasheema and me are ecstatic when we look at ourselves in the mirror. She's only four and I am fourteen. We hold each other smiling.

Keep moving. Then I am already around the corner from school while the bus pulls away with Laura still on it because she has fallen asleep in her seat and nobody has bothered to touch her.

On the corner of Prospect Ave. and East 167th Street where the bus lets me out, I see Rakeem waiting for me. I am not supposed to really know he's there for me and he is not supposed to show it. He is opening a Pixie Stick candy and then he fixes his droopy pants so that they are hanging off the edge of his butt. I can see Christian Dior undies. When I come nearer he throws the Pixie Stick on the ground next to the other garbage and gives me his hand just like any B-Crew-Boy would do when he saw his other crew member. Only we are not B-Crew members, we get run over by the B-Crew.

He says, Yo, man, did you find Layla?

I nod and listen to what he is really saying.

Rakeem says, Do you know that I got into Math 3? Did you

hear that shit? Ain't that some good shit?

He smiles and hits me on the back and he lets his hand stay there.

I say, See what I told you before, Rakeem? You really got it in you to move on. You doing all right, man.

He grunts and looks at his sneakers. Last year the B-Crew boys tried to steal them from him but Rakeem screamed at them that he had AIDS from his cousin and they ran away rubbing their hands on the sides of the buildings on the Grand Concourse.

Rakeem says, Man, I don't have nothing in me except my brain that tells me: Nigger, first thing get your ass up in school. Make them know you can do it.

I say, Rakeem, you are smart, man! I wish I had your smart. I would be going places if I did.

He says, And then, Lorrie, I got to get people to like me and to stop seeing me. I just want them to think they like me. So I got to hide *me* for a while. Then you watch, Lorrie, man: *much* people will be on my side!

I say to him, Rakeem, you got Layla and baby Tee Tee and all the teachers on your side. And you got smart. You have it made.

He answers me after he fixes his droopy pants again so that they are hanging off exactly the middle of his ass: Man, they are whack! You know what I would like to do right now, Lorrie? You know what I would like? Shit, I ain't seen you since you went back to school and since I went back. Hell, you know what I would like? But it ain't happening 'cause you think Ima look at my cousin Layla and her bastard and love them and that will be enough. But it will never be enough.

I think about sitting on his lap. I did it before but then I let months go by because it was under the Bruckner Expressway and I believed it could only last a few minutes. It was not like the kind of love when I had the kids because I believed they would last forever.

He walks backwards away and when he gets to the corner, he starts running. No one else is on the street. He shouts, Rocky's Pizza! Ima be behind there, man. We got school fooled. This is the master plan. Ima be there, Lorrie! *Be there.*

I want to tell Rakeem that I have missed him and that I will not be there but he is gone. The kids are enough. The words are important. They are all enough.

The front of Jane Addams is gray-green with windows with gates over all of them. I am on the outside.

The bell rings first period and I am smiling at Mr. D'Angelo and feeling like this won't be a complete waste of a day. The sun has hit the windows of Jane Addams and there is even heat around our books. Mr. D'Angelo notices me but looks away. Brandy Bailey, who doesn't miss a thing, announces so that only us three will hear: Sometimes when a man's been married long he needs to experience a new kind of loving, ain't that what you think, Lorrie?

For that she gets thrown out of the classroom and an extra day of in-school suspension. All ears are now on me and Mr. D'Angelo. I am beyond feeling but I know he isn't. And that makes me happy in a way, like today ain't going to be a complete waste of a day.

He wipes his forehead with an imported handkerchief. He starts out saying, Class, what do we remember about the piston, the stem, and the insects? He gets into his questions and his perspiration stops and in two minutes he is free of me.

And I'm thinking: Why couldn't anything ever happen, why does every day start out one way hopeful but then point to the fact that ain't nothing ever going to happen? The people here at school call me ugly, for one. I know I got bug eyes and I know I am not someone who lovely things ever happen to, but I ask you: Doesn't the heart count? Love is a pie and I am lucky enough to have almost every flavor in mine. Mr. D'Angelo turns away from my desk and announces a surprise quiz and everybody groans and it is a sea of general unhappiness but no one is more than me, knowing that nothing will ever happen the way I'd like it to, not this flavor of the pie. And I am thinking: Mr. D'Angelo, do you know that I would give anything to be like you, what with all your smarts and words and you know how to make the people here laugh and they love you. And I would give anything if you would ask me to sit on your lap and ask me to bite into your ear so that it tingles like the bell that rips me in and out of your class. I would give anything. Love is a pie. Didn't you know that? Mr. D'Angelo, I am in silent love in a loud body.

So don't turn away. *Sweat.*

Mrs. Cabrini pulls me aside and whispers, My dear Lorrie, when are you ever going to pass this City Wide? You certainly have the brains. And I know that your intelligence will take you far, will open new worlds for you. Put your mind to your dreams, my dear boy, and you will achieve them. You are your own universe, you are your own shooting star.

People 'round my way know me as Lorrie and the name stays. Cousin Cee Cee says the name fits and she smacks her gum in my face whenever she mentions that. She also adds that if anyone ever wants to kick my ass, she'll just stand around and watch because a male with my name and who likes it just deserves to be watched when whipped.

Ma named me for someone else. My real name is Lawrence Lincoln Jefferson Adams. It's the name on my school records. It's the name Ma says I got to put on my application to college when the time comes. She knows I been failing these City Wide Tests and that's why she wants to practice words with me every day. She laughs when I get them wrong but she's afraid I won't learn them on my own, so she asks me to practice them with her and I do. Not every day, but a whole lot: look them up and pronounce them. Last Tuesday: Independence. Chagrin. Symbolism. Nomenclature. Filament. On Wednesday, only: Apocrypha. Ma says they have to be proper words with proper meanings from a dictionary. You got to say them right. This is important if you want to reach your destiny, Ma says.

Like for instance the word *Library.* All my life I been saying that "Liberry." And even though I knew it was a place to read and do your studying, I still couldn't call it right. Do you see what I mean? I'm about doing things, you see, *finally* doing things right.

Cousin Cee Cee always says, What you learning all that shit for? Don't you know it takes more than looking up words to get into a college, even a damn community college? Practicing words like that! Is you a complete asshole?

And her two kids, Byron and Elizabeth, come into the kitchen and ask me to teach them the words too, but Cee Cee says it will hurt their eyes to be doing all that reading and besides they are only eight and nine. When she is not around I give them words with up to ten letters, then they go back to TV with the other kids.

When we have a good word sitting, me and Ma, she smooths my face with her hands and calls me Lawrence, My Fine Boy. She says, You are on your way to good things. You just got to do things the proper way.

We kiss each other. Her hands are like the maid in the movies. I know I am taken care of.

Zenzile Jones passes me a note in History of Civilization. It's the part where Ptolemy lets everyone know the world is round. Before I open it, I look at her four desks away and I remember the night when I went out for baby diapers and cereal and found her crying in front of a fire hydrant. I let her cry on my shoulder. I told her that her father was a sick man for sucking on her like that.

The note says, Please give me a chance.

Estine Smith, my mother's sister who wants me and the kids to call her by both names, can't get out of her past. Sometimes I try on her clothes when I'm with the kids and we're playing dress-up. My favorite dress is her blue organza without the back. I seen Estine Smith wear this during the daytime and I fell in love with it. I also admired her for wearing a dress with the back out in the day, but it was only a ten-second admiration. Because then she opens her mouth and she is forever in her past. Her favorite time to make us all go back to is when they lynched her husband, David Saul Smith, from a tree in 1986 and called the TV station to come and get a look. She can't let us go one day without reminding us in words. I never want to be like her, ever. Everybody cries when they are in her words because they feel sorry for her, and Estine Smith is not someone but a walking hainted house.

. . .

Third period. I start dreaming about the kids while the others are standing in line to use the power saw. I love to dream about the kids. They are the only others who think I am beautiful besides Ma and Anita. They are my favorite flavor of the pie, even if I got others in my mind.

Most of the time there are eight but when my other aunt, Samantha, comes over I got three more. Samantha cries in the kitchen and shows Ma her blue marks and it seems like her crying will go on forever. Me, I want to take the kids' minds away. We go into Ma's room where there is the TV and we sing songs like "Old Gray Mare" and "Bingo Was His Name O" or new ones like "Why You Treat Me So Bad?" and "I Try to Let Go." Or else I teach them Math 4. Or else I turn on the TV so they can watch Bugs or He-Man and so I can get their ironing done.

Me, I love me some kids. I need me some kids.

Joe Smalls talks to me in what I know is a friendly way. The others in Woodworking for You don't know that. They are like the rest of the people who see me and hear the action and latch on.

Joe Smalls says, Lorrie, man, that bitch Tareen got half the percentage problems wrong. Shit. Be glad you don't have to deal with no dumb-ass Tareen bitch. She nearly got my ass a F in Math 3.

I get a sad look on my face, understanding, but it's a fake look because I'm feeling the rest of the ears on us, latching, readying. I pause to Heaven. I am thinking I wish Ma had taught me how to pray. But she doesn't believe in God.

Junior Sims says, Why you talking that shit, Joe, man? Lorrie don't ever worry about bitches!

Perry Samson says, No, Lorrie never ever thinks about pussy as a matter of fact. Never ever.

Franklin says, Hey, Lorrie, man, tell me what you think about, then? What can be better than figuring out how you going to get that hole, man? Tell me what?

Mr. Samuels, the teacher, turns off the power saw just when it gets to Barney Moore's turn. He has heard the laughter from underneath the saw's screeching. Everybody gets quiet. His face is like a piece of lumber. Mr. Samuels is never soft. He doesn't fail me even though I don't do any cutting or measuring or shellacking. He wants me the hell out of there.

And after the saw is turned off, Mr. Samuels, for the first time in the world, starts laughing. The absolute first time. And everybody joins in because they are afraid of this and I laugh too because I'm hoping all the ears will go off me.

Mr. Samuels is laughing Haw Haw like he's from the country. Haw Haw. Haw Haw. His face is red. Everyone cools down and is just smiling now.

Then he says, Class, don't mess with the only *girl* we got in here!

Now it's laughter again.

Daniel Fibbs says, Yeah, Mr. Samuels is *on*!

Franklin laughs, No fags allowed, you better take your sissy ass out of here less you want me to cut it into four pieces.

Joe Smalls is quiet and looking out the window.

Junior Sims laughs, Come back when you start fucking bitches!

Keep moving, keep moving.

I pick up my red bag and wade towards the door. My instinct is the only thing that's working, and it is leading me back to Biology. But first out the room. Inside me there is really nothing except for Ma's voice: *Don't let them boys.* But inside there is nothing else. My bones and my brain and my heart would just crumble if it wasn't for that swirling wind of nothing in me that keeps me moving and moving.

Perry laughs, I didn't know Mr. Samuels was from the South.

With his eyelashes, Rakeem swept the edges of my face. He let me know they were beautiful to him. His face went in a circle around mine and dipped in my eyes and dipped in my mouth. He traveled me to a quiet place where his hands were the oars and I drifted off to sleep. The thin bars of the shopping cart where I was sitting in made grooves in my back, but it was like they were rows of tender fingers inviting me to stay. The roar of the trucks was a lullaby.

Layla Jackson comes running up to me but it's only fourth period because she wants to try and talk some sense into Tyrone. She hands me little Tee Tee. Tyrone makes like he wants to come over and touch the baby but instead he flattens his back against the wall to listen to Layla. I watch as she oozes him. In a minute they are tongue-kissing. Because they are the only two people who will kiss each other. Everyone says that they gave themselves AIDS and now have to kiss each other because there ain't no one else. People walk past them and don't even notice that he has his hand up her shirt, squeezing the kickball.

Tee Tee likes to be in my arms. I like for him to be there.

The ladies were always buying all kinds of fruits and vegetables for their families underneath the Bruckner Expressway. They all talked Spanish and made the sign of the cross and asked God for forgiveness and gossiped.

Rakeem hickeyed my neck. We were underneath the concrete bridge supports and I had my hands on the handle of a broken shopping cart, where I was sitting. Don't go back, Rakeem was telling me, don't go back. And he whispered in my ear. And I thought of all the words I had been practicing, and how I was planning to pass that City Wide. Don't go back, he sang, and he sat me on his lap and he moved me around there. They don't need *you*, he said, and *you* don't need *them*.

But I do, I told him.

This feeling can last forever, he said.

No, it can't, I said, but I wound up leaving school for six months anyway. That shopping cart was my school.

I am thinking: It will never be more. I hold Tee Tee carefully because he is asleep on my shoulder and I go to catch the BX 17 back to my building.

Estine Smith stays in her past and that is where things are like nails. I want to tell her to always wear her blue organza without the back. If you can escape, why don't you all the time? You could dance and fling your arms and maybe even feel love from some direction. You would not perish. *You* could be free.

When I am around and she puts us in her past in her words, she tells me that if I hada twitched my ass down there like I do here, they woulda hung me up just by my black balls.

. . .

The last day Rakeem and I were together, I told him I wanted to go back, to school, to everyone. The words, I tried to explain about the words to Rakeem. I could welcome him into my world if he wanted me to. Hey, wasn't there enough room for him and me and the words?

Hell no, he shouted, and all the Spanish women turned around and stared at us. He shouted, You are an ugly-ass bastard who will always be hated big time and I don't care what you do; this is where your world begins and this is where your world will end. Fuck you. You are a pussy, man. Get the hell out my face.

Ma is waiting for me at the front door, wringing her hands. She says it's good that I am home because there is trouble with Tommy again and I need to watch him and the kids while she goes out to bring Lula Jean home from the movies, which is where she goes when she plans on leaving Tommy. They got four kids here and if Lula Jean leaves, I might have to drop out of school again because she doesn't want to be tied to anything that has Tommy's stamp on it.

I set Tee Tee down next to Tommy on the sofa bed where I usually sleep. Tommy wakes up and says, Hey, man, who you bringing to visit me?

I go into the kitchen to fix him some tea and get the kids' lunch ready. Sheniqua is playing the doctor and trying to fix up Shawn, who always has to have an operation when she is the doctor. They come into the kitchen to hug my legs and then they go back in the living room.

Tommy sips his tea and says, Who was that chick this morning, Lorrie, man?

I say I don't know. I begin to fold his clothes.

Tommy says, Man, you don't know these bitches out here nowadays. You want to show them love, a good time, and a real deep part of yourself and all they do is not appreciate it and try to make your life miserable.

He says, Well, at least I got Lula. Now that's some woman.

And he is asleep. Sheniqua and her brother Willis come in and ask me if I will teach them Math 4 tonight. Aunt Estine rolls into the bedroom and asks me why do I feel the need to take care of this bum, and then she hits her head on the doorframe. She is clicking her heels. She asks, Why do we women feel we always need to teach them? They ain't going to learn the right way. They ain't going to learn shit. That's why we always so alone. Click, click.

The words I will learn before Ma comes home are: Soliloquy, Disenfranchise, Catechism. I know she will be proud. This morning before I left she told me she would make me a turkey dinner with all the trimmings if I learned four new words tonight. I take out my dictionary but then the kids come in and want me to give them a bath and baby Tee Tee has a fever and is throwing up all over the place. I look at the words and suddenly I know I will know them without studying.

And I realize this in the bathroom and then again a few minutes later when Layla Jackson comes in cursing because she got a 60 on the Humanities quiz. She holds Tee but she doesn't touch him. She thinks Tyrone may be going to some group where he is meeting other sick girls and she doesn't want to be alone. She curses and cries, curses and cries. She asks me why things have to be so fucked. Her braids are coming undone and I tell her that I will tighten them up for her. That makes Layla Jackson stop crying. She says, And to top it off, Rakeem is a shit. He promised me he wouldn't say nothing but now that he's back in school he is broadcasting my shit all over the place. And that makes nobody like me. And that makes nobody want to touch me.

I put my arm around Layla. Soon her crying stops and she is thinking about something else.

But me, I know these new words and the old words without looking at them, without the dictionary, without Ma's hands on my head. Lasheema and Tata come in and want their hair to be like Layla's and they bring in the Vaseline and sit around my feet like shoes. Tommy wakes up still in sleep and shouts, Lula, get your ass on in here. Then he falls back to sleep.

Because I know I will always be able to say the words on my own. I can do the words on my own and that is what matters. I have this flavor of the pie and I will always have it. Here in this kitchen I was always safe, learning the words till my eyes hurt. The words are in my heart.

Ma comes in and shoves Lula Jean into a kitchen chair. She says, Kids, make room for your cousin, go in the other room and tell Tommy to get his lame ass out here. Layla, you can get your ass out of here and don't bring it back no more with this child sick out his mind, do your 'ho'ing somewhere out on the street where you belong. Tommy, since when I need to tell you how to treat your wife? You are a stupid heel. Learn how to be a man.

Everybody leaves and Ma changes.

She says, I ain't forgot that special dinner for you, baby. I'm glad you're safe and sound here with me. Let's practice later.

I tell her, Okay, Ma, but I got to go meet Rakeem first.

She looks at me in shock and then out the corner of my eye I can tell she wants me to say no, I'll stay, I won't go to him. Because she knows.

But I'm getting my coat on and Ma has got what will be tears on her face because she can't say no and she can't ask any questions. Keep moving.

And I am thinking of Rocky's Pizza and how I will be when I get there and how I will be when I get home. Because I am coming back home. And I am going to school tomorrow. I know the words, and I can tell them to Rakeem and I can share what I know. Now he may be ready. I want him to say to me in his mind: Please give me a chance. And I know that behind Rocky's Pizza is the only place where I don't have to keep moving. Where there is not just air in me that keeps me from crumbling, but blood and meat and strong bones and feelings. I will be me for a few minutes behind Rocky's Pizza and I don't care if it's just a few minutes. I pat my hair down in the mirror next to the kitchen door. I take Anita's letter knife out my jacket pocket and leave it on the table next to where Tommy is standing telling his wife that she never knew what love was till she met him and why does she have to be like that, talking about leaving him and shit? You keep going that way and you won't ever know how to keep a man, bitch.

Obscenity

*"Obscenity" is often not an expression by an individual uttered
under great stress and condemned as bad taste, but one
permitted and even prescribed by society.*
—E. E. Evans-Pritchard, British social
anthropologist, 1925

Among the Ba-Ila
("among" as if swarming
the petri dish of the British
Imperialist), there exist

expressions used collectively,
that is, in the presence
of women and children,
in fact, in chorus

since these obscenities
are sung, not scrawled
across a riverbank
where innocent boaters

of Victorian persuasion
might encounter them.
"His great penis is a size!
A thing without end!

It must have a long unwinding!"
The female mourner's song,
the trot a little arch
as if the words themselves

could make the gored warrior
rise in tumescence. Or sometimes

it's just what they do
with their hands, singing,

writes the patrician scientist
who considered obscenity
a privilege, a way to spur
routine labor with ardor,

or to invoke life
at the moment of death. I drag in
the anthropological so one can reject
the paradigm of the primitive,

we, who have no physical labor
which requires our neighbor,
nor sustained interest in creation—
except in art, that work to ward off

death. There will always be
those in the boat who slow down,
who listen and transcribe
in their tiny script.

Public Works

How, in summer, a man and woman,
as in Paris, embrace under trees,
and the leaves and the grass
bend back and sweat

amends them, in a park where
the squirrels eat well, where
the bronze horse could heave off
its officer. How it is like water,

sex in summer. You cover
yourself, your leaves rippling,
the sun inside. In Calcutta,
Omdurman, even Paris, the bent

grass curls and dies and birds
take it away until slums root,
the trees bare in smooth hard lust.
Touching a man there as if no one

but the exiles espaliered
to the bare walls watched,
just the occasional touch. How,
at the far end another bronze

beckons, her robes folded over
children and jugs of water,
and Haitians pass her by, hands clasped,
walking home into

the dark. How the roundness
of their faces shines as leaves, not money.
How, when the general dismounts,
swords fall from the arches,

speeches sigh from the trees,
and his first words to her
are what's carved in
by the ghostlike, lovestruck loiterers.

Recessional

When I think of you, you disappear in stages,
As if I were paralyzed below my heart
And wore, like a blanket, a thousand pages
Of you on my lap, who come apart
In the slightest wind, and disperse
Like leaves. I trade you for the universe,
Which holds me back
When I lean over to gather up and restack
Your laughter and your temperature.

The more I think of you, the fewer
Opportunities remain, as if a painted
Memory could not contain you, and you set yourself
  down in pastel,
Fleshed out like a Degas bather—demanding of, yet
  tainted
By, the light I need to see you well.

And still, what can I do but accept this theft
Of woman from man?—until all that is left
Is a sadness like unnaked bodies in the dark on a bed,
Neither touching nor asleep, and neither comforted.

Coconut Don Fu Delight

On the Schuylkill Expressway,
in the midst of a snarl of traffic,
a truck from N.Y.C. pulled up
alongside, with red filigree
appearing through a film of grit

in swirls like an ice cream sundae:
"Coconut Don Fu Delight,"
the fading billboard explained,
evoking "tasteless bean curd
with a white chewy sweetness

of caramelized coconut,"
alleviating swelter-
ing heat and stalled vehicles,
and perhaps that car owner
whose left front tire flew across

clear to a highway divider,
hitting radio traffic news.
Coconut Don Fu Delight
on any day, especially
the present one, awaiting

the cool chill of autumn.
Last fall, Hato told me of
his proposed trip to China
to find and marry a girl
met through correspondence school.

My wife and I asked, Why not seek
a Japanese American,

but we sensed the difficulty
of trying to marry someone
who would be like a sister,

the fish pond being so small,
desire and need and difference
not able to bind with sameness
into a lasting mat woven
to support a generation

equal to his grandma's spunk
which rode a boat, survived a war,
withstood matched marriage, loved ones' deaths,
and drove Hato's brothers and him
to make progress towards their dreams.

At the age of eighty-three,
with a new pacemaker in her heart,
Grandma pumped her exercycle
and fed all four boys before school.
Grandma passed, but memory

must have impelled Hato to write
to Hong Kong, to Indonesia,
to China, until one response
was left after filtering.
"I want you to feel my bosoms

heaving with the thought of you."
A glossy photo with soft focus
revealed a girl who looked undressed,
through her clothes. I felt steam rising
between a mesh of desire.

I know those girls in Guangzhou,
or rather their skirts hiked high
above their knees on bicycles,

deflecting off car fenders
like schools of fish turning corners

on city streets flanked by signs
of economic progress.
A Party official said:
"Once the window is open,
it's hard to keep the flies out."

This girl wanted much to leave.
Let's call her Annabelle Wong
who had a family friend
write words that made Hato's head spin
so that he took this journey

to this faraway country
without knowing the language
or geography, thinking
Guangzhou was next to Beijing.
We tried to dissuade Hato

who had to go anyway
and returned without knowing
whether he had been married
by the government in Beijing.
Hato then entered a blue funk,

color of his VW bug
with shiny chrome and sparkle paint
that carried him through blizzards
and others of life's events.
I thought I had him when he said:

It's just like when he was driving
and he could only perceive through
a small patch he cleared with his glove;
he knew he had to stop the machine.
But Hato wouldn't or could not stop;

he sponsored Wong to San Francisco,
took her to Reno for some fun,
then flew to Philadelphia.
But she wished to visit a friend
in the Bronx—Hato took her there,

and Wong disappeared. Every once
in a while, she still corresponds.
She is cultivating bean curd
in a basement, sifting and sifting.
When will the ripening begin?

from A Reluctant Education

I was raised to be a virgin until I married. Not that anyone ever said this to me directly. Such a general truth didn't need to be spelled out. It never seriously crossed my mind, in high school, to go all the way. I had boyfriends with whom I made out, madly, but I was saving myself for marriage. For a girl like me, virginity was the Big Given, the monumental monolithic Given from which all the other givens sprang. The whole social structure balanced delicately on that thin membrane. If I couldn't have sex until marriage, that dictated quite nicely that I would marry, sooner rather than later, no doubt, and that I would be a wife, and as night follows day, a mother. Virgin; wife; mother. It was all I knew, and all I needed to know.

I had a boyfriend my sophomore year of college who wanted to marry me. After we graduated, of course. We were both enrolled in small private schools in North Carolina, his for boys, mine for girls (we were not yet men and women). Unlike me, Bill already knew what he wanted to be: an orthopedic surgeon. His father was an orthopedic surgeon. We sort of assumed I would be a high school English teacher, if I had to be anything at all.

What Bill and I had in common, besides our profound youth, was a great desire to please our parents. My parents loved Bill Nelson. He was everything they hoped for in a future son-in-law. I loved Bill Nelson—at least I thought I did. I loved it that he matched my parents' expectations, which I still assumed were my own. I was highly sensitive to what my parents and, by extension, society expected of me. I was well aware of what was valued, acceptable, respectable, approved. Bill fit the bill. We were nineteen and smug. Orthopedic surgeon. Orthopedic-surgeon-wife-and-mother.

The moment came, however, when I threw it all over. I can't say exactly why. It was like those Frankenstein monster stories, where a heretofore lifeless form suddenly springs to life and takes over.

This was the moment when my real self made herself known, and her first word was "no."

The breath of life, the spark that ignited this deadened, sleeping self, was Bill's parents' French Provincial living-room furniture. We were driving somewhere in his little white Skylark convertible (there was a plastic rose on the antenna, a romantic touch). Bill was telling me how his parents were going to give us their French Provincial living-room furniture when we got married. I had never seen this furniture, and so he described it to me in detail—the curved legs of the sofa and chairs, the cool blue of the upholstery, the pale coffee table. I was sure it was quite nice. A vision came into my mind, of Bill and me lounging around on his parents' French Provincial living-room furniture in our future married life. This was supposed to be a beautiful scenario for a girl like me.

But suddenly, I didn't want it. I didn't want it, *no!* I didn't want it at all. I didn't want his parents' French Provincial living-room furniture, I didn't want married bliss, and most of all, I didn't want Bill.

Nothing had ever been so clear to me. I couldn't wait to get away from him. I almost jumped out of the car. Of course I rode on, demurely, but in my heart I was already gone.

It took several weeks to break up with him. After all, nothing really had happened; it wasn't anything he *did.* It was hard on my parents. I couldn't say, when Bill and my parents, teary-eyed, asked me why I didn't love him anymore. I just didn't. In fact, I could hardly stand to be around him, though out of common decency I made myself pretend he wasn't loathsome to me. I was shocked at myself, but there was no getting around what I really felt: I couldn't wait for the day when Bill—and all he represented—would be out of my life forever.

It was, as they say, a turning point. I told my parents that I wanted to transfer to the University of North Carolina at Chapel Hill, because it had a writing program. I had gone my first two years of college to a school that didn't offer any creative writing courses. I was doing what I was supposed to do, what was expected of me. I had always wanted to write, but it had never occurred to me that I could be a writer. I was groomed for more modest, conventional dreams. I was bored to death by them, but I didn't even know that I was bored. Boredom was too sophisticated a concept for me, and besides, it wouldn't have been *nice* to be bored.

I had first visited Chapel Hill on a computer date. The girls at our college filled out computer questionnaires for a fee, and were matched with boys at neighboring schools. My date at Chapel Hill was an intense young man, a philosophy major, with beautiful dark hair and eyes, quite a bit on the ethereal side. I found him irresistible, which he did not find me, but he was nice to me, and showed me around. I had not known that there were places big enough in the world to lose oneself: to become anonymous. I was used to everyone knowing my business, which, I began to sense uneasily, was rapidly coming to be to lose my virginity. I sensed, like the tadpole, that I was about to transmogrify, and I wanted a pond big enough to do it in. I felt strange twitchings in my extremities, odd internal pushings.

Of course losing my virginity was no easy matter for me. I'm sure there were plenty of young men at Chapel Hill who would have been pleased to relieve me of my burden, but I was not about to lay aside lightly the most fundamental tenet of my life. I had the additional problem of equating sex not with love or passion, but with morality. I had been raised Southern Baptist, after all.

I spent that first fall at Chapel Hill reading about Situation Ethics and the New Morality. Still, more and more often, I found myself in strange scenes with a changing cast of boys. Despite the various settings, these situations had in common someone's hand down someone's pants. Still, I wrestled with my virginity like B'rer Rabbit with Tar Baby.

Once I almost did it, almost gave myself to an art student who had taken me out in the woods near a dam in the country. At the last moment he confessed he had a girlfriend. How shaken I had been! I had almost done the wrong thing with the wrong person at the wrong time for the wrong reasons. Still, it would have been a relief to have it over with, once and for all.

At the end of the school year, I didn't go home for the summer, but stayed on campus, ostensibly to take a course. When the

Southern summer rolled in, like a big wave, knocking everyone over, I took to spreading myself out on the hard concrete by the campus pool. I gave myself up to Fate, and soon enough, along it came in a pair of thin, white gym shorts.

The first view I had of destiny was a hairy leg right beside my face when I opened my eyes after falling asleep one particularly hot day by the pool. For a moment I thought I was seeing not a person's leg at all, but that of some strange animal I couldn't identify. The man to whom this leg belonged stooped down beside me, breathing very hard, and sweating; his musky odor penetrated even the chlorine air around the pool. When finally I looked in his face, I saw big white teeth grinning at me, like the wolf in Little Red Riding Hood, all interest and appetite.

Beside the pool, the man's white German shepherd was crouched down on his front legs, his hindquarters raised indelicately in the air, lapping the chlorine water. I had seen the two of them often, the man and the dog, moving across campus with the same motions. I had never seen the dog go to other people, like normal friendly dogs, or bother with other animals, for that matter. He was always loping along with his nose close to the ground, as if he were searching for something, and everything else were just in the way.

"I've seen you around," the man said, and he grinned at me with his big white teeth.

I was surprised. That anyone—that he—should have noticed me. But maybe it was the bohemian clothes I had started to wear, black tops and Indian print skirts. It was easy to look bohemian when all the other coeds wore Villager shirtwaists and Weejuns. At the beginning of the summer I had taken an apartment by myself. It was 1968, the first year the university would allow girls to live off-campus. That made me something of a bohemian, too. Anything to separate myself from the sticky mass of Southern girls who clung together like honeybees in the dorm.

"Hey, Wolfgang! Here!" the man called, and the dog came loping to where he stooped. I tried to pet it, but it moved away from me and regarded me with its yellow neutral eyes.

"I'm afraid he's not the friendly sort," the man said, burying his fingers deep in the stiff white fur. "Why don't you have dinner with me tonight?"

My mind went into action, processing a polite excuse. Instead I said, "Why not?," surprising myself.

"Good!" the man said. "Good! Good!"

His name was Joel Goldetski, and his occupation, campus politico. He was twenty-six years old, Jewish, had sinus trouble, and had dropped out of graduate school in political science to agitate. All this he told me in a great laughing way, but I had trouble getting the joke, fearing it was on me. He was dark where I was fair, masculine where I was feminine, Northern where I was Southern. He drove a beat-up old Lincoln full of white dog hair and books, and in the back seat I noticed a ratty blanket, full of significance. He didn't help me with my door.

We drove to his place because he wanted to take a shower. It was a basement apartment in a row of cheap concrete block buildings of washed-out watercolors. There was a mattress on the floor, books piled everywhere, and one poster on the wall, of Lenin.

When he emerged from the bathroom, he was wearing another pair of shorts, hardly anything at all. For dinner he fixed a cheese omelette, and we drank cheap bittersweet wine out of coffee mugs. I had never met anyone who talked like Joel. It wasn't just his accent. It was his *words*. There were so many of them, all nasal and Northern and fast. I could hardly follow the sense of things, but it didn't seem to matter. I couldn't take my mind off his big white teeth.

When eventually we found ourselves in bed, and I, naked, waxed uncertain, Joel didn't try to persuade me. He got up to take another shower, leaving me alone in bed with the sound of water running. I was used to a little more in the way of pressure; the lack of drama was a letdown. When Joel got back in bed, he had on striped pajamas and began to read the newspaper. He wore black-rimmed glasses to read. After he finished the editorials, he turned out the light, climbed on top of me, and we did it.

I tried to stay awake to record the momentous event in my memory. But actually, there had been very little to remember. Cars were going by above our heads on the street, and occasionally the beams would flash through like search lights. I wondered if my landlady would realize I hadn't come in that night. She would *know*. I fell asleep with the thought that I had changed my life.

Sometime in the night, I woke with a terrible start and sat straight up in bed. First I was aware of being afraid, then I remembered where I was, and then I remembered the dream. My parents had driven from my hometown in South Carolina to the university. They had known exactly where to find me, and they had burst into Joel's room. The dream gave me a sick feeling. Beside me, Joel was snoring in an ungodly fashion. Maybe he would expire, and I would be left to explain to the police. When I couldn't stand it another moment, I reached over and turned his head to the other side, away from me. I couldn't get back to sleep. I imagined roaches crawling on the cement walls. It was odd to be lying so close to the floor; Joel was not into creature comforts. I stared into the darkness, wondering if I had ruined my life. Maybe I would get lice.

But in the light of day, I was in love. I liked everything about Joel, even the hair in his nose. He was my first lover, which, I told myself, was romantic in and of itself. We went out to breakfast at the Pineroom. It had dark wood booths, played classical music, and the people there smoked pipes, wore beards, and played chess. I felt very adult having scrambled eggs in public the morning after I'd spent the whole night in bed with a man. Joel was older and darker than anyone I knew. I looked back on the little blond Southern boys on whose fraternity beds I had wiggled in girlish indecision with disdain. I had left them in the dust.

I contemplated how suddenly, overnight, everything had changed. I no longer had to get married. Marriage was the big domino that would knock over all the other dominoes in my life, and now, I didn't have to push it.

There was the question of contraceptives. I certainly didn't want to get pregnant. My whole girlhood had been about not getting pregnant. Babies before marriage ruined if not your life then certainly your reputation, possibly more important. Joel would pull out at the crucial time but that was nerve-wracking. I understood that I was supposed to be responsible for not getting pregnant. I made an appointment at the campus infirmary. I debated over whether to make up a story about being engaged. It was not for nothing that I had had an ethics course. I knew in the same way I knew I was supposed to wait until marriage that the infirmary wouldn't give the pill to unmarried girls.

Dr. Griffin came into the little room where I was waiting, and shook my cold hand. "Now what can I do for you?" he asked, taking his seat behind the desk. He had on a white coat, which matched his white hair. He was old enough to be Father Time.

"I'd like to go on the pill," I said in a tiny voice.

He gave me a benevolent smile. Everybody loves a bride. "I see. Are you engaged, then, my dear?" He was making a notation in my folder.

"No, sir."

"I see. Bad cramps, maybe?"

"No sir. It's just that...I...I...I..." I couldn't think exactly how to word it. "I'm having intercourse, and I need a contraceptive." I blushed so deeply the top of my head tingled.

He stopped writing and eyed me for a long time across the polished wood, contemplatively, as if he had just now noticed me. "I see," he said at last, though I wasn't sure he saw at all. Absentmindedly I checked through the buttons on my blouse to make sure they were buttoned. "As you must know," he said, "this university has a policy against giving the pill to unmarried girls. It just isn't done. I imagine in a few years—by 1970, even—it will be routine. But for now that's the policy, and I'm required to go along with it." He paused thoughtfully. "I'm sure many girls who come in here make up a story about getting married, and then we do help them. If you see what I mean."

We both sat in silence while I thought this over.

"Well, thanks anyway," I said, my throat aching. I fell into a deep study of my skirt.

"Do you mind telling me why you chose not to?"

It was hard to find the words. My voice halted. "Because if I lied, it would make what I'm doing seem wrong. And I don't believe it is wrong. I can't explain it very well."

"I think you explain it very well," Dr. Griffin said. He leaned back in his chair, fingertips one on one. "I respect your position. It shows integrity."

My hand quivered in my lap.

"I can give you the name of a doctor in town," he said, "who might be able to help you out. I don't know how he feels about these things, but he's a good man. And I wish you luck." Then he stood and shook my hand.

Joel was waiting for me in the Pineroom. When I sat down, I couldn't help beaming. I held up the piece of paper.

"Ha," Joel said. "The prescription."

"As good as. It's the name of a doctor in town who can fix me up. The infirmary won't give pills to unmarried girls."

"Sometimes I forget about the South," Joel sighed. "Until you remind me."

I didn't quite understand what he meant. I had hardly been out of the Carolinas, and then mainly with my family on trips to visit relatives in Texas. Philadelphia, which was where Joel was from, might have been another planet. Joel spoke differently from me; he acted differently. I liked to think of him as a dark, romantic stranger, but sometimes, like when he blew his nose, he didn't seem quite romantic enough. And besides, he never told me he loved me and something in me kept waiting. Sometimes he acted too much like an older brother. He stood on the sidelines and waved encouragement to me, but beyond that, he didn't help me. He wouldn't carry the ball of my life, no matter how often I indicated to him that I wanted to toss it his way.

I made an appointment with the doctor in town. The nurse had me slide almost off the table, spread my legs, and put my bare feet on the cold metal stirrups. I hardly saw the doctor, for as soon as he came in, he sat on a stool between my legs, and the sheet hiked up by my knees was like a tent he was crawling into. What in the world was he doing in there? I felt odd sensations of discomfort, but the feelings were hard to locate, identify. It was embarrassing to have the nurse stand there while the doctor kept saying in a petulant voice, "Relax, relax." He meant muscles, not feelings.

After the exam I told him what I had told Dr. Griffin.

"Do your mother and father know about this?!" he exploded. "Did they bring you up to act this way?! Did they? Did they?"

I couldn't speak. Tears clotted my throat, but he wouldn't make me cry, he wouldn't, wouldn't.

"I have three girls myself, and I pray to God that when they get to be your age, they have the sense to save themselves for marriage. What have you got to look forward to now? And think how disappointed your husband will be! Think how *he'll* feel."

Angrily he scribbled out a prescription. "I guess I have to give you this. It's not against the law. There's no use getting pregnant on top of all this. But I'm not in the business of giving out contraceptives, so don't go telling all your little friends they can come here to get them." And with that, he swept from the room.

I had to use the sheet to wipe a big wet tear off my cheek.

I drove over to Joel's apartment that evening and found him cooking spaghetti in his gym shorts. He was so familiar and foreign to me. I sat at the table and burst into tears. When I was able to see again, there was his leg resting on the rung of the chair, and I remembered the first time I had met him.

"So tell me," he said nasally, in his accent.

"The doctor fussed at me. He said what would my parents say. He had no right to do that! No right to talk to me that way!"

"Good!" Joel said. "Good! That's the first time I've heard you mention your rights. Did you tell him to shove it?"

I looked at him, shocked. "What do you mean? I could never do a thing like that! I couldn't even speak! It's for you I'm doing all this!"

He sat down, grinning at me with his big white teeth. He was the only person I knew who brushed his teeth in the shower. "Oh, it's for me, is it? It is, huh? I didn't realize it was such a sacrifice." And he reached over and touched my breast. He was always doing unexpected, Northern things.

"I'm not like you," I said. "You can tell anybody off. Words come easy to you. I know you're older and smarter than me. Just don't tease me."

"Not smarter," he said. "Just older. Older, dear Paulette, because there was never anyone as young as you." Then he stood and took me in his arms, as if he really did love me.

. . .

I had lost my virginity, I had changed my life, but I had to admit that sex was a disappointment. The first thrill of going all the way (where?) had worn off, and now I felt like a bystander, watching someone else get something, but what? Joel seemed to get exactly what he wanted out of it, but in my own body I felt inarticulate, dumb. I didn't even have the first idea what it would say if my body could speak, in its own language. (I was twenty-one years old, and I didn't know that women had orgasms. Did other girls like me know about orgasms? This is the sort of question that needs to be asked at high school reunions.)

I couldn't get used to sleeping with Joel and his snoring, and I was homesick for my own bed. I was spending nearly every night with Joel, in his bed, and when I returned to my own apartment, it had the appearance of a life suspended. One night, I dreamed that two people I had known in high school were getting married. Everyone from school was there for the wedding. The couple had eyes that were just alike, huge and bronze. Everyone could see that they belonged together. As the wedding festivities were going on, in the dream I felt an unutterable sadness, and when I awoke the next morning, the feeling lingered on.

I started the pill, and at the end of the month, when it was time for my period, it didn't come. Joel was organizing a strike of underpaid local black people at the cafeteria, and I was seeing less and less of him. The previous spring, Martin Luther King had been assassinated. When I had heard of King's death, I came bursting into my dorm room. My roommate was lying in bed reading a magazine. She was engaged to an airline pilot, and took courses called Kiddie Art and Kiddie Lit. Yes, she had heard. "But what did you expect?" she said to me. "It was bound to happen sooner or later. I don't see why you're so upset." And she had gone back to reading her magazine.

Now I went here and there, too restless to sit still. I felt I had a slight fever all the time. My mind was electrified, I had a hard time making my body keep up with it. To make myself a little independent from my parents, I took a part-time job handing out towels at the gym. It didn't seem right to take their money when they would have died if they knew what I was doing. I avoided thinking about that as much as possible. I have to lead my own life, I would say to Joel, as if that were in doubt.

When I told him about missing my period, he insisted on a pregnancy test. On the way to the hospital, my sample bottle of urine in hand, I felt I had come to the worst day of my life. Anybody having a pregnancy test should be happily married with an extra bedroom. The test came out negative, and when I spoke to Dr. Griffin, he said the pill had probably affected my cycle, and to wait another month. Though I knew better, I felt I had gotten what I deserved.

At the end of the summer, I went home for my older sister's wedding. The wedding was like a Cecil B. DeMille movie. It was as if, for her whole life, my mother had been preparing for this masterpiece of detail no one else cared about. All the food, clothes, parties, and people made me sleepy and tense. I kept to myself as much as possible. My back ached the whole time, and I feared I had injured it somehow, lying unmarried under Joel Goldetski.

When I returned to campus in the fall, Joel did not get in touch with me, and though I was shocked, I had expected it. I felt very tragic for a few weeks, abandoned and all, but after a while I slept with another boy and then another, feeling very cavalier and complicated. Sometimes I would see Joel and the big white dog moving across campus in the old way. I would look away then, for there was something in the dog, the way he ran searching so, that reminded me of myself. Once there was a picture of Joel in the campus newspaper. He had been hit over the head with a bottle at a campus demonstration against the Vietnam War. For a while I tried to rouse the proper emotions regarding him—outrage, anger, hurt—but these were hard to sustain. After a while I wasn't sure who had left whom, or why. It was just that the summer had come to an end.

I moved into a one-bedroom apartment in an old house and worked long weekends at a little table near a window above a yard. I was writing stories, and it took a lot of my time. Everything around me moved, and I moved, people came and went, I ran searching and didn't know what I wanted to find. In the spring, I fell in love with a junior English major who wanted to be a lawyer, and I thought, This is it, finally, this is love, and it will last forever. But then I received a fellowship to graduate school at a university all the way across the country, and in spite of love, I knew I would be moving on, perhaps for a long time to come.

Summer, & Her Painted Flowers

She is all definition, the woman, her summer
Dress pleated with sweat.

In the firm prow of her belly, in the hold
Her cargo settles
In, as if to stay.

When it comes she will be flat
Which is herself again,

Another.

Outside dry grasses nudge each other *as if
to say*

Lie still again, then.
(All of the angles make sense to the wind.)

Everything here is animal is quick
To touch and soft to bite.
The man will die.

All of the eyes in back of him are women's eyes.

For now, though, look
How tenderly she holds his head, magnificent,
    immense,
Tipped like a beggar's soft wool cap.

It's hard for him.
It takes both of them to hold it.

What a field her mouth makes

On his. All of the eyes. All of the ways
He's seen, women see.

It Is Hard to Look at What We Came
to Think We'd Come to See

Everybody knew what you were going to do before you did it.

You couldn't go out without encountering
Some version of yourself, oh, years old
You thought you had let go of,
Like that narrow hall, the row of frames
Contiguous along the wall, you walk down,

walk down.

> Look, here are crows the way a child draws them, urgent m's
their wings extended
> and the earth's a gorgeous proof
> of insanity, that bright kinetic wheat.
korenveld met kraaien. You wanted those hard k's,
> the sky's
> blue fingerprints you could almost identify
as if what Van Gogh saw and what he saw with
> made the same terrible strokes.
These crows have no eyes, no need and if they had
> would close, close up.

The frames are down
And sunlight nails onto the wall
Explicit shapes "... AS SIMPLY SHAPE ...
Liberated windows, no view into,

out of.

Of Da Vinci's Cartoon, the expert said,
"If I had a painting this torn I'd trash it."

He can't restore
                    the picture the man
         mad at
who knows what
              shot holes in.
Later you were still there
... NOT AS DESCRIPTION,

                         NOT AS REMINISCENCE," the way sudden
Birds aren't birds but the configuration
Fear wakens.

He can't make the picture whole again.
He makes damage the thing we look for
              because it's there...
                             look now
what breaks... it is like this
              everywhere
                             ...becomes

the reason
         we come to look.

Venetian Blinds

*...these blinds give people control over light; they let the outside
in and still allow a feeling of privacy in a glassed room.*
—from a brochure on window treatments

you say what I remember
didn't happen

and hanging the blinds
I admit my dreams swerve

from rippled instants
to serial repeats

I think about the smooth surface
of belief   and begin to accept

your version   but
there are those swift branches

over car windows   the sun
dazzling

in and out of quick shade
our focus hard on the road

till only a trance
could keep me safe

you were driving too fast
was it Montana   the Canadian Rockies

seeing the deer I braced
for braking and none came

my hand clutched your arm
then the fawn sprang

only one ticked sound
a joint popping

the strobed glare   dizzy
passing through us

and I wanted to stop
looked back

at the road straight
behind us   alarm

met suddenly with blankness
and you wouldn't

you claim there was no fawn
but there's a knowledge deep as marrow

the memory won't recede
and when your words shutter it

into doubt light still seeps
watery through slats

and I have wondered if
you would try to deceive me

why you wouldn't go back
how you forced the return

for evidence into the kind of dream
where light is psychedelic

and we take chances
if we look too deep

Twos

The rooms where you entertained me are open to view
And expensive now. But I'm drawn that way.

The sea steps ashore up wide ascents of marble.
Corinthian columns ruffle like bedclothes.

Rough side of a towel, smooth side of silk.
Your mare's-tails unravel, and cloud the royal blue.

A brown Raleigh three-speed. A wide-tired Schwinn.
Bricks glow, air whirls, horizon wheels up gray.

I leaf into a lane, thirsting for cloudburst.
You're wet, like a gardenia.

I speak bright plumage.
Your breeze blows in.

Who Burns for the Perfection of Paper

At sixteen, I worked after high school hours
at a printing plant
that manufactured legal pads:
Yellow paper
stacked seven feet high
and leaning
as I slipped cardboard
between the pages,
then brushed red glue
up and down the stack.
No gloves: fingertips required
for the perfection of paper,
smoothing the exact rectangle.
Sluggish by 9 p.m., the hands
would slide along suddenly sharp paper,
and gather slits thinner than the crevices
of the skin, hidden.
Then the glue would sting,
hands oozing
till both palms burned
at the punchclock.

Ten years later, in law school,
I knew that every legal pad
was glued with the sting of hidden cuts,
that every open lawbook
was a pair of hands
upturned and burning.

PATRICK SYLVAIN

Creativity and Fire

I am struggling with the first line.
No, those words will not fit in my mouth.

Language is neutral,
the speaker is not.

I can start fire with words,
the pen is like a boxer's gloves.

I could dance this tropical dance with you,
but my eyes are watching the lines

carved underneath your eyes
like waves or horizons.

The world is a dangerous place,
Bush's words and actions made it real.

One death after another,
I breathe fear

people cough black smoke in Baghdad's doorways.
As war rises, my throat utters silence,

I'll do battles with words,
where is my dictionary?

I was only looking for a line,
to fish out a map of faces.

Now, I feel the pulsing of words
drumming on the surface of my tongue.

Language is a volcano's rim,
the speaker is the fire.

Doo-Bop

I thought you were through,
but like good sex,
you keep coming back. Miles,
what's up with Doo-Bop?

When I listen to you,
I hear a car crash,
a voice reaching climax,
a flock of birds with metal wings
aiming for the moon.

Your ears danced,
when street movements
float through your window.
Hip-Hop, Rap. Lick your mouthpiece,
finger the valves, blow.

Until the bell echoes,
mimicking the sounds from:
Car horns, homegirls' talk,
hands embracing hips,
brothers jiving,
footsteps of mortals,
and shouts of raw temper
crawling to your window like a spider.

Shoo-Wop,
Bop,
Be-Bop,
Hip-Hop,
Rap,
Jazz,
Doo-Bop,
your music, Miles,

is a bridge,
a red liquid
flowing in my brain.

Now, go ahead,
dip the chip into chocolate.
Lick,
finger,
let the brew blow,
a high-speed chase,
a sexual ecstasy,
a boxer with a split-second punch.
Sometimes, your trumpet
is a feather
brushing a nipple.

Horizon of Gun Butts

The history of my country is
in every link of chains
at the foot of Boukman's copper statue
overlooking a dusty town
at the depth of despair
with candlelights of anger
burning in every tired palm.

Low black clouds converted light
into darkness, the man with a fat cigar
stands in front of the black mirror,
at Palais National where he plunders dreams
silently. Leaving only rocks
and drifting dust behind.

The iceberg of nightmares are melting
in our imprisoned minds as we journey
along the horizon of gun butts,
sticks and chains.

One by one, we are starting
to pull our shadows away
from burning cages.
There's a new man in the mirror
he holds a clock which is slowly ticking
like a dying breath.

His eyes and fat hands are
desperately searching for our dreams.
The sun is slowly conquering low black clouds
to establish a permanent noon.

Father Scarmark—World War I Hero— and Democracy

The black uncombed wig with stiff grotesque braids
sits atop his broad and pockmarked forehead;
and his grip on the dull tomahawk is almost woman-
like. Yes, Father Scarmark's winsome eyes
and slouched spine do not befit a proven warrior.
But the beaded American flag designs on the bayonet
scabbard symbolize breaths stolen from German officers.
Back then he was called "Master Check" because he made
sure captured officers died mysteriously from minor
wounds during pauses in the artillery fire.

Today Father Scarmark is a chronic worrier; his tears
radiate eerily from the inside corners of his eyes.
He says he can vividly recall trench warfare.
We have been taught to distinguish that each
campaign has its own unique choking emanation.
But we have yet to understand what the Foggy
Dawn revealed: measurements of sanity?
And the eviscerated remains of young,
unsuspecting adversaries? He knows other
far more gruesome elements, as does his family.
They know the intimate details through the crude
odor that sometimes surfaces from the dilated pores
of his sweaty body.

And the long johns under his old-time dance outfit
are fiery red. In his armpit, almost hidden by
the mirrored arm bustles, is the Bible he helped
translate into our mother tongue. They say
Scarmark's resurrection and pathologic vengeance
began when he was taken prisoner. This was early on.

There are stories he was maimed at parties of the German
echelon. Others say he was kept alive on boiled rodents.

Fate arrived one afternoon as he was attempting
suicide. An artillery round landed above the bunker
at the exact moment he hung himself. In the fiery
dust that followed, as the crudely fashioned noose
locked in tight braid-increments around his neck,
a page from *Gee-je-sa, Jesus* floated toward him
like a harmless moth and remained stationary,
long enough for him to read about the criminals
who were nailed beside Christ. Once he begged
for His forgiveness, the rope unloosened itself
and rose mysteriously to the ceiling and burned
in the shape of the crucifix. Although the fire
went out, its ethereal shape was imprinted in
the European air.

Today "Father J. Scarmark"—as his name reads
on the deteriorating mission door—has this phantom
transfiguration painted on the church.
"*Ma ni ke mi ne qwi ya ni be be ma te si wa ni.*
This is what gave me my life" is the painting's title.
It is marveled at by the few daring white people
who stop at the mission on their sightseeing scurry
through the Settlement.

Although he speaks in repetitions and clichés,
Father Scarmark gets incensed if family members
mock his unoriginality. Under the grotesque black
wig, his family recited, should be stamped:
"Boastful War Hero." Yet few in the tribe can
match his deeds. Over supper he is known to say:
"*I ni ye to ki we tti mi ya ne ne mi ya tti.*
E we ta se i wa ni. That is probably the reason
they are jealous of me. Since I am a proven
veteran. *A qwi ke e ma ma to mo ne ni wi ya ni.*
And not because I am a religious man."

But the male heirs knew differently.
Especially Scarmark the Second.
"Bravery in war has nothing to do with it,"
he once told his brothers who always
held his judgments in reserve.
But he went on and they listened
to the shrewd history of Black Eagle Child
politics: it was their father who formed
the 1923 Business Council after tampering
with the ballot boxes. At issue was democracy—
the one-person, one-vote concept. Unfortunately,
their father's father had raped and murdered
a young woman, Dorothy Black Heron;
and the county authorities offered to forget
the crime if the Scarmark patriarch agreed
to become a federally recognized Chief
and allow education into the tribe.
When their father saw his father step
perfectly into his own moccasin tracks,
at the scene, there was no choice but
to burn the pivotal vote.

From there on out, American Indians
as practicing Democrats and Republicans
became a literal myth. That single,
incinerated vote, as would be seen by scholars
later on, initiated the arduous rock-strewn
journey toward our demise. Every jagged edge
stabbed our sensitive feet and we became
hobble-legged. Mandatory education
for tribal youth was enacted by the State
of Iowa at the expense of "Heron Dorothy Black."
Often their father would openly reflect (long before
the sons could fathom the implications of the story)
that had the election swung for sacred, traditional
chieftainship the "Cigarstore Indian" days

would have returned. It was well-known most
youth fled to the hills in short-lived protest.
When food and water supplies were depleted
they came out to federal truant officers
who patiently herded them to the barn stalls
for the wicked and cultural disfiguring.

Summer Tripe Dream and Concrete Leaves

1.

There exists a future when green trees will be extinct.
In our ingenuity artificial tree factories—A.T.F.'s—
    will flourish.

Far ahead I see myself walking under one,
and I grow uneasy at the thought of chunks
of painted concrete swaying in the man-made
breeze from bark-textured iron rods.

Don't worry, says the regional safety inspector,
they can withstand mega-knot winds.
Plus they've got internal warning mechanisms
with stress signals linked to monolithic fans
in the western part of the state. Should a fracture
occur, the fans are automatically programmed
to slow down.

Bullshit, I think as white dust and chips
of paint blow about in the false wind,
stippling my indolent face.

2.

Inside the honeycomb-lined tripe intestine
there is a woman held captive, and I am there with her.

She resembles Debra Winger, the Hollywood actress.
She sits on my lap undressed and allows me to explore
her smooth virginal skin, her sensuousness.
Outside of her bone frame and beyond the newborn,
translucent skin, she cries. Together we hear herself.

The fine designs on the walls and the terraced floors
begin to tremble. One end of the floor begins to surge
like an ocean wave and it travels beneath—
and lifts us upward, speeding toward
consciousness.

Paper Garden

B ack in the days when life was easy and you could walk down the street at night and not worry about anybody knocking you over the head with some blunt object and taking all of your pocket change, Miss Mamie Jamison, the neighborhood kids' godmother who gave us money and candy and let us hide in her parlor when the big boys chased us from the playground, took seriously ill one summer and had to be put to bed. Her daughter, the one all the way from New York, moved in with her, dressed in nothing but what looked like black bodysuits and tall fruit-basket hats like that Chiquita woman wears on banana peels. If it wasn't black bodysuits, she was wearing a pair of men's trousers and shirt along with a mighty fine pair of work boots. But despite her icky clothes, she looked like a movie star from the silent screens: deep, dark black hair, thin red lips, and that pale, powdery skin color, like she was waiting for some invisible director to yell "Action!" and give her the go-ahead to say her lines like that was the only thing God created her for.

Of course, the only reason the Chiquita woman, Miss Marion, wasn't talked about like a dog too much by the other ladies in the neighborhood was because she *was* from New York. Meaning, Miss Marion obviously knew what the latest fashions were, and knew much more about fads and styles than these country women, including my own mama, would ever know in their whole lifetime. Which was also why she was called "Miss" Marion, even by the old folks—the way she spoke, calling everybody "darling" and "sweetie" and always saying how much she loved somebody, even complete strangers she met walking down the street. You would have thought they were blood relatives.

My mama was the main gofer over Miss Marion; she would come home just about every other day with some catchy word or phrase that she had heard Miss Marion say, or what someone else had heard her say. Once, while leaving out the door to go to a

Daughters of the Confederate Army meeting, Mama said to Papa and me, "I'll be back in about an hour. Chow." And when she closed the door, Papa, with a puzzled look on his face, looked up from his evening paper and asked me, "What dog?"

Something was happening to the town of Harper. All the women wanted to be Miss Marion, ordering just about every dress and hat and scarf and shoe that the Sears, Roebuck catalog had to offer. Even the men, down to the youngest and up to the oldest, watched Miss Marion out of the corner of their eyes. We watched how she swished her way through town knowing full well everybody was looking at her in a skirt that was at least ten inches too short and ten years ahead of Harper's time. Eddie T., who claimed he was blind, sat on that old tree stump at the end of the main street playing his harmonica, wrote and sang a song about her that teetered on the edge of vulgarity, sometimes drawing a good crowd if it was a Saturday and a nice pile of spending money in his ragged hat that he kept between his feet.

Even Papa, whenever he saw Miss Marion coming up on our side of the sidewalk, all of a sudden had to go check the oil in the car, or he had to go clip the hedges, or the grass was too tall and he had to go cut it. I think Mama knew what Papa was up to, but it was summer and it was hot and the price of ground beef had dropped and life was just too wonderful so Mama didn't say anything. "At least he's away from that paper," she said. It was true: Papa had about three weeks' worth of *Harper's Sentinels* piled up on the coffee table. Most times now, he spent looking out the big picture window.

It wasn't long before Miss Marion had announced that she would start giving acting lessons down at the community center, since she had some acting degree from NYU and saw that it was not only a good deed but "an absolute duty"—another one of her catchy phrases that she almost wore out—that she bring some of her "expertise" back home to those who weren't as fortunate as her.

So, to be honest, I wasn't in the least bit surprised when I came home from playing kickball with Terry and Kicky, and Mama asked me if I was planning to take any acting lessons from Miss Marion—as if we had already discussed it before.

"I thought you were going to play football this summer, Sonny Buck?" Papa asked me, not even giving my head the chance to let the first question sink in good.

"And what's wrong with acting lessons?" Mama asked Papa in that tone of voice that said you best watch what you say.

And Papa caught the hint, so he shuffled around in his favorite chair, the one that sits in front of the television set, then he lowered his newspaper just enough so we could see his eyes. "There's nothing wrong with taking acting lessons if that's what Sonny Buck wants to do. I just thought maybe he wanted to play football since he's been playing for the last three summers."

"Well, missing football this year is not going to kill him none. I think it will do you some good to expand your culture, Sonny Buck. I'll give you ten dollars." Then she gave Papa that look that told him that he had better not bid against her. And when he didn't, she said, "Good. Now that's settled. The class starts Monday."

I looked over at Papa, but he was already behind his paper again. So there I was.

But it wasn't bad. Come to find out, all the mothers in the neighborhood—except for Kicky's mama—made their kids go see Miss Marion for acting lessons, which consisted mainly of remembering some line from a Shakespeare play and reciting it while she shouted how you should be standing, or lecturing you on the proper facial expression, or having fits on when you should be breathing. And if you weren't doing it just right, she would just get all undone: flapping her arms, twisting her face, then sometimes dropping to her knees and saying: "Lord, please help me educate these ignorant people." That ignorant part was something we didn't feature too well and Debra Ann told her so, being since Debra Ann was brought up that way; that is, brought up to cuss grown folks out and not think twice about it.

But Miss Marion took an interest in me. She didn't yell when I read, but watched me with her mouth hanging open, telling everybody to knock off the noise back there—mainly Terry and another boy we called Scootie who could make funny noises with his armpits. Miss Marion said that I was talented.

What she say that for? I recited Shakespeare for Mama and

Papa almost every evening before, during, and after dinner. Papa said that I was real good. Mama said I was a born actor. A genius was the word Miss Robbins—the school's English teacher who doubled as the drama coach in the springtime—used one night when she came over just to hear me read a few lines from *A Midsummer Night's Dream*. I was good. No lie. I imagined myself going to Hollywood, or to New York like Miss Marion, and becoming a real actor like James Cagney or Humphrey Bogart and star in films where I get to shoot the bad guy and run off with his dame because he's nothing but a big gorilla and she had been giving me the eye all along at the bar between sippings of tequilas and straight shots of brandy. I was Othello hanging upside down from a big tree in our front yard; I was Romeo on the football field. At the groceries: Puck. At the gas station with Papa: Macbeth. Then Henry VIII, then Hamlet, then King Lear, and I couldn't stop. Terry and Kicky couldn't keep up and came close to hating me, something I couldn't blame them for. I was crazy. I figured if I didn't make it in pro football, at least I had my acting talents to fall back on.

But the gist of this story really didn't kick in until about a month later, a July evening. Terry and Kicky were over my house for dinner: Terry was fat and would eat anything that couldn't get up and run; but Mama was always inviting Kicky over because she said Kicky was from a dysfunctioning family on account of his daddy been to jail about ten times and his mama was always hooking up with somebody who was going to Memphis for a couple of days. So, sometimes, if Kicky didn't eat with us, he didn't eat.

"So, how's the acting coming along?" Papa asked Terry and me.

Terry, between mouthfuls of some hot meatball dish—a recipe Mama got from Miss Marion: "It's okay. We studying *Romeo and Juliet*. Can I have some water?"

"Oh, that's nice," Mama said. "I remember in the springtime the senior class would always put on *Romeo and Juliet* out on the front lawn of the school. That's how we paid for the prom every year. I was Juliet. We decorated the whole stage with honeysuckles and white clovers and I wore a crown of white roses." Mama smiled. "I was beautiful then."

Papa said, "What do you mean? You're still beautiful."

Mama looked up at Papa, just like everybody else at the table did. I remember one time he was telling everybody down at the lodge how his boy was going to make the football team and go on to play for some Ivy League school. But I remember getting cut the first week of tryouts, so I hid out over Kicky's house all day long. It didn't do any good, Papa knew exactly where I was because Debra Ann told him out of spite on account of me not wanting to carry her books after school. When he found me, he said, "Let's go home, Sonny Buck," and the way he said it I knew I had let him down. At home Papa got on the phone and called an emergency meeting being since he was sort of like the vice-president of the lodge. He told me to come with him. When we got there all the men were fussing and wondering what was so important. Then Papa said, "This is my son, William 'Sonny Buck' Jackson, and he didn't make the Little League football team. If he never makes any other team in his life, he's still my boy and I love him. And if any of you say anything out of pocket I'll bust your damn noses." Then we went down to Olive Branch and he bought me a beer at Tang's. Papa said not to say anything about the nose busting or the beer drinking, being since he was sort of like a deacon at church. That was the only time I ever remember Papa saying or doing something profound and not being behind his paper.

At the table, Mama put her napkin up to her face and dabbed at the corner of her eyes. "Frank, you're so kind. I love you. I love you all." Then she got up and went around the table kissing everybody. Just like Miss Marion, except Mama wasn't performing. Even Kicky probably wanted to cry; I don't think he had ever been kissed by his mother.

And right then and there I made a vow that if ever the moon and the sun and all the constellations ever decided to twist, switch up, collide, or explode in the heavens and cause me to lose my mind and want to run away from home, I was going to take these two beloved people with me.

After dinner, Mama told me to take a plate of rum muffins over to Miss Marion. She told Kicky and Terry to go with me, but they suddenly claimed to hear their mothers calling them. So I had to

go by myself. I picked up the plate and said "Chow" to everybody.

When I got to the house, I was standing in an open doorway.
"Miss Marion?" I peeped in, looking into a dark living room full
of bulky antique furniture, the stench of Vick's Vapor Rub and
the confined, wet, musty smell, like after a long, hot summer
rain—and it crept out on the porch with me and tingled my
nose. "Miss Marion?" I repeated.

"William, is that you?"

I peeped farther into the room and saw a figure move in a chair
over there in a corner. "Yes, this is me."

"Well, why you out there? Come in here."

I walked in, bumped into something, and she clicked on a table
lamp.

She had been drinking. She wasn't wearing a hat. Her hair was
down and she was more white than usual except for her eyes:
bloodshot and veiny red-like.

"You okay, Miss Marion?"

"I couldn't be better," she said slowly, then she brought a glass
up to her mouth and sipped.

I stood there watching, not knowing what to do, but then I
remembered why I had come. "My mama sent you these." I held
the plate out in front of me. "She made rum muffins."

She laughed. "That's all I need." She downed the rest of her
drink. Then she frowned up at me like I was something awful.
"Do you know how evil the world is?"

"Excuse me?" I asked, steady holding onto the plate of muffins
because I was too nervous to do anything else.

"The world is full of evil. You knew that, didn't you?"

"Ahh...yes, I knew that."

"But you know, I don't think anybody else knows about this
world but me and you." She burped. "I don't think most folks
know they're mean. If they don't know any better, how do you
expect them to act good? You see what I'm saying, William?"

"Yes, I think so."

"You know what bad thing I did one time? I made this fat girl
cry. When I was up in New York, I went to this restaurant with
this friend of mine and he brought his girlfriend with him. She

was as big as a house. I don't know what Judd saw in her. She must've pissed Jack Daniels. I don't know. Anyway, I think I was drinking, I can't remember, but I remember telling this girl that I bet she eats a lot. Then Judd tells me that she's a vegetarian. A vegetarian. Can you believe that, William? A three-hundred-pound vegetarian?"

I shook my head no.

"I couldn't believe it either. So I ask him what in the hell has his vegetarian been snacking on? A damn California redwood? I thought it was funny but she started crying and Judd was trying to hush her up because everybody was looking at us. The more she cried, the louder I got, until they put all of us out of the restaurant. They didn't have good food anyway. But now I feel so bad about what I said. I got to tell everybody what I've done. That's my punishment." She grabbed some tissues from a roll of toilet paper and dabbed at her eyes and blew her nose. "You know, I think this world would be a lot better place to live if everyone would just do as I say. Know what I'm talking about, William?"

"Miss Marion," I hesitated, "are you drunk?"

"Not yet, but I have the potential of becoming an outstanding alcoholic. You just give me time."

I didn't say a word. I picked up the roll of toilet paper and tore some off, and out of nervousness started playing with it as Miss Marion was steady talking—mainly about how much money her mama had spent on her education and now she can't even find an acting job off-Broadway. I twisted the paper—tucking it here, pulling it there, twisting the bottom—until finally, I had created a little flower, something between a carnation or a rose, but a nice-looking flower just the same. We both looked down at the object in my hand; I think I was more surprised.

She took the flower from me and started crying. "You know what this is, William?"

"A paper flower?"

"No," between sobs, "this is beauty. Painful beauty. You're just like me. You can look right through pain and see the beauty of it. This is painful beauty. Thank you, William."

I was ready to go home. I tried to throw a hint by moving closer to the door and shuffling my feet like I suddenly heard someone calling my name.

"Sit down, William," she said, handing me the roll of paper. She refilled her glass, then leaned back on the couch. "You got it, William."

"Got what, Miss Marion?" I asked, steady making the paper flowers.

"It! You got that third eye right here"—she tapped her forehead—"and you can see right down that narrow line. I can't see that line as clearly as I want to. I never seen anybody read Shakespeare like you can. How do you do it? You ain't got to answer that. Most folks who are good at something usually don't know how they do it."

Since it wasn't a big roll, I had quickly made about twenty flowers and they were on the floor around my feet.

Miss Marion dropped to her knees and ran her fingers through the flowers like they were gold coins. "These are beautiful." Then, like a sudden afterthought: "I'll be back. I got to go check on Mama."

She disappeared down the dark hallway, leaving me alone in the parlor. I was trying to decide whether to leave, figuring that she was too drunk to remember whether I was here or not, but that wouldn't be a proper thing to do. By the time I had made up my mind to make a break for the door, Miss Marion came back with a flashlight and two new rolls of toilet paper.

"Mama's doing just fine. Let's go."

"Where we going?"

Miss Marion looked at me like I had a hole in my head. "Outside. We're going to plant these beautiful flowers in the garden. You don't actually think that I'm going to let all these flowers just multiply inside my house, do you?"

Though it was late, about eight or nine, it was still hot. Miss Marion started digging small holes in the empty garden with her fingers. She placed a flower in the hole and then she mashed the soft dirt around the paper stem. She was quiet, working quickly, stopping every once in a while to take a sip from the bottle that she had brought out here, or to grab some more paper flowers from me, or to tell me where to shine the flashlight. This went on for about an hour until we had the whole flower bed in the front yard covered in paper flowers.

Miss Marion started crying again. "This is just damn lovely!"

We stood there in the night looking at the paper garden. It really did look nice.

"You know, William, some things are just too good for this world." Then she looked up at me like she was expecting me to add to what she had just said. But I kept my eyes on the garden.

Fortunately, I heard Papa calling me and I told Miss Marion that I had to go. I started running down the street, pushing what she had said off to the side somewhere.

She yelled, "Goodbye, William! Come back in the morning and we can see how beautiful this garden looks in the daylight!"

"Okay," I yelled, running wildly in the middle of the street like I had just been set free out of a cage, looking back only once just in time to see her wave at me and take another sip.

But the next day it rained, a thunderstorm so terrible that even Mama said, "Maybe you shouldn't go to class today, Sonny Buck. Miss Marion will understand." I sat in the house all day until the rain stopped about early evening.

Later I walked down to Miss Marion's house and stood in front of the paper garden. The rain had melted the flowers and the only thing that was left was soggy toilet paper all over the yard. I stared at the garden for a long time.

I knocked on the door, but there wasn't an answer. I peeped through the windows into the parlor, but I didn't see anything. Once, I thought I saw Miss Marion ducking down the dark hallway, but I wasn't sure. I knocked on the door and yelled her name, but there was no answer. I went home.

Suddenly, everything changed. Not a change back, not a change forward, but a change like the closing scene of a play when the curtain comes down and you wonder were you really there. Like the melting of the paper garden was an omen of what was to happen next: Miss Mamie Jamison died toward the end of the summer. She was buried the next day, then the next day after that Miss Marion packed up everything in the middle of the night and left, and not too long after that the house was boarded up. Just like that. Then slowly Harper went back to the way it was: boring. Like a rubberband, Harper had stretched to accommodate one of its own, then quickly snapped back into place—nothing different, but the same. My mother went back to her meatloaf on Mondays, spaghetti on Tuesdays, and pork chops, chicken, roast, noodles, and stew on the other days. I went back to my football practices, and Papa slipped back behind his paper.

Once, I wondered if Miss Marion was a real person, or if she was one of those fallen angels who comes to earth to earn her wings. You would wonder about anybody who steps into your life and charms and dazzles you, forces your imagination to soar higher than the heavens, then for no reason, quietly disappears, never realizing that someone has been left behind whose love for life is now running on an uncontrollable high. Though it didn't last long, but for one brief moment in my life, I wasn't William "Sonny Buck" Jackson, the junior varsity football player. Instead, I was William "Sonny Buck" Jackson, the Broadway star, the Hollywood actor—the whole town not the town, but a stage; the townspeople not the townspeople, but the audience. Maybe Miss Marion knew what she was doing and was just giving me a taste of what could be, letting me know that there's a different world outside the four walls of Harper.

I wondered what had become of Miss Marion. I imagined myself traveling from town to town, city to city, looking for a Miss Marion. Stories would spring up about me, about some kid looking for a friend that he met one summer. Toothless old men with guitars will be moaning some sad song about lost friendship and loneliness and how cruel the world can get without a good friend or a faithful dog. I will become a legend. Of course, some folks will say I never existed, but just somebody's crazy imagination gone wild. But that wouldn't get me down, since worrying about that kind of stuff doesn't bother me none anyway.

Shoeshine

1.

For the one on top,
polished, sartorial,
but abstracted as Lincoln
on his Memorial,
fingers tapping
the armrests, or flapping
his newspaper,
time at this connecting stop
slows like winter on a mink-oiled
Little Leaguer's glove...
When each shoe is stripped,
finally, of its upper
layers of the world, a silver-
gold coin will appear
at each tip,
in which he will apprehend
some reflection of himself, a type
of license to renew his step
for the next leg of his trip.

2.

The one on his knees
snapping the cloth back
and forth, could make, if needed,
a two-stick
fire for food or heat,
and as he shoulders
into his work,
the slightest toehold
of light does take,

over which he huddles
as if to shield
from the wind those least sparks.
His cloth gains speed
until it is itself a blaze
and then with a noise
like a pop the shoes
are complete and they move
down and away, dark
soles flashing below the fading heels.

When McCorkle Is Working
on the Rail

on the Baltimore
and Ohio Railroad—wheels
of the train
clacking
and clicking

I wish it could
be rhythm

on a drum
or church piano

something
for the
folks
to remember of
working men

& Mr. McCorkle
Redcap
porter
dishwasher
peach brown
lemon yaller
black tall
and fat working
men with
those smoking
& sweet smelling
lips life saver mint
smelling tobacco loving

lips of a working man
saying yes to rye
whiskey good morning
to me   honey and ma'am
to the ladies

McCorkle
served sandwiches
and coffee
hustled
with a shine
rag (made old
shoes shine

and smile like
new) a working
man Redcap
porter
with the dignity
of a butler
a preacher

skin
so fine
he made
you smile

Redcap/porter
razor
sharp & clean
Negro   a
spirited
man

a door held open
as it should be
for your
mother   sister

and sometimes
you—McCorkle Gentleman's
Gentleman   working
on the railroad

Before the Beat

Like that answer written on a trip
that after makes no sense,
we remember before birth, but cannot
force it to the clumsy breath
of this wet hurt of a joy
we are now.
So let that big boy go
and find your tribe to ride with.
We spilled the apple juice long ago.

I remember brontosaurus.
A growing rain of dinosaurs now
flattens every green and red song.
A slow game future plays with itself.
We carbon copies keep trying our luck,
trying on different duds,
just God tricking ourselves out of
boredom. Fancy Solitaire. Enjoy.
We must forget to remember.
Every body knows.

Flotation Device

Peeking for hours into the fire,
I find the faces staring back—
marching cities rise and fall.
Still as stone I sit,
practicing death.
My machine of flesh hangs lightly.
Our body's noise keeps us sleeping.
Later we arise into dreams,
and awake to Jacob's ladder.
At death we graduate.
There the slow-mo stomp of dinosaurs roars
through the whir of saucers or seraphim's wings.
Here there are no more stars.
We become our dreams, and they
are heavens or hells of
no return.
A slow, thick thud of blood's body, Maya,
holds us safe prisoner in second chances
for now, though,
so let's begin the brightest nightmare
that ever rocks God's all-night café!
Awake the eternity in each second.

JACK RIDL

In the Last Seconds

Coach looks at the scoreboard,
tries again to press another loss
in the backcourt of his brain.
The players feel their blood quiet,
return to its common wander.
The fans shake their heads
like tired dogs, put on their coats,
hats, gloves, leave the bleachers,
head back to what's always there.
The cops shrug, step outside.
The vendor starts counting the till.
In the parking lot, the attendants wave
their red flashlights, the snow sparkling
in the crossing beams of the headlights
of those who left before the end.
Coach's wife looks at her hands.
Coach's daughter stares
into the rafters, listens
to the words of blame, pretends
they are dead leaves caught in the air.
The manager sacks the towels.
The assistant thinks again of a way
he can land a head coach's job.
The custodian stands at the locker room door,
ready to remind the players
to hang up everything before they leave.

Night Gym

The gym is closed, locked
for the night. Through
the windows, a quiet
beam from the streetlights
lies across center court.
The darkness wraps itself
around the trophies, lies
softly on the coach's desk,
settles in the corners.
A few mice scratch
under the stands, at
the door of the concession booth.
The night wind rattles
the glass in the front doors.
The furnace, reliable
as grace, sends its steady
warmth through the rafters,
under the bleachers, down
the halls, into the offices
and locker rooms. Outside,
the snow falls, swirls, piles
up against the entrance.

Poetry Night

The poetry club in Jean's neighborhood scheduled readings of new works every Wednesday in the basement of a popular restaurant, The Two Bruce Café. A surprising lot of people showed up regularly to hear and then critique the week's artistic efforts, and the two lawyers named Bruce who owned the place felt rewarded because the audience was hungry afterwards and stayed to eat.

This Wednesday, a few days before Easter, the club was featuring Harriet Marriott's latest poems about incest and Arthur M. Armlicher's poems about such matters as the lead in drinking water and salmonella in eggs. Jean's husband didn't think it would be entertaining, so she arranged to meet Claude and Edith, two of their unmarried friends. Although she often argued with him about their responsibility to the community, Jean's husband didn't like listening to words without music and most Wednesdays stayed home, playing board games on his portable computer and watching Court TV.

Soon before showtime, it started to rain. The Two Bruce Café was a short walk, and it was only a light rain, really a drizzle, but Jean dressed in a raincoat, rain hat, rain boots, and carried an umbrella in her satchel just in case. Jean didn't like getting wet. Her husband asked if Jean had her keys, if she had fed the cat, and if there was a honeydew melon in the trunk of the car. The answer was yes, straight down the line.

Winter or summer, they ate melon for breakfast, honeydew (Jean's favorite) or cantaloupe. Over the years, Jean had selected so many melons, she always expected to score a good one, but her judgment didn't always work. She squeezed, smelled, and stroked a melon, looking for a certain scent, the bounce of ripeness, golden veins in the cantaloupes, and in the honeydews, a squeaky surface with a texture like washable silk. Still, melons can be disappointing, hard or tasteless, particularly in winter, when they import them in an unripe state from a distant land, like Peru. The latest melon was in that who-knows category, and Jean had left it in the trunk of the car in the hope that it might ripen better with a few extra hours in a warm snug place. "I'll get the melon on a jury break," her husband said with some relish. He loved the rain.

Jean arrived at The Two Bruce Café early, and bought a fancy bottled sparkling water at the bar. Brendan, the bartender, referred to it as "dreadful Welsh water," and he was pouring it into a wineglass when Jean's attention was diverted by a bearded face. She stared right through the man's thick eyeglasses into his eyes. They had no mirth. They had no fire. They reflected no opinion at all. They were pale blue plates. Jean was transfixed. Then she was flustered. She had stared too long. "You remind me of someone I know," she tried to explain. "I thought you were him." He extended his hand. "My name is Zemmis," he said. "Can I sit with you?" Jean flinched at the speed of his demand. She had no desire to be impolite, but no time either to think of an excuse. Her smile was overly bright. "Actually," she said, "I'm meeting friends."

Jean gave Brendan three dollars for the glass of water, and carried it downstairs to the basement, where she picked out a small round table with three chairs. Seeing Zemmis right behind her, she laid an object on each chair (her rain hat, her umbrella, and her scarf) to indicate that she was saving the seats. She looked up to meet Zemmis's blank blue eyes. "Why don't you sit here?" Jean said, pointing to the adjacent table, as if she were a real-estate agent touting a fine neighboring island, surrounded by its own unique stretch of air. Zemmis sat down.

"Are you a poet?" she asked across their new boundary. She was still smiling too hard. "Yes," Zemmis replied. "Professional?" They both laughed at the idea of writing poetry for a living. "I've had some poems published," he said, and Jean didn't ask where. "I'm also a potter," he said. "I just came from a ceramics class."

Jean's bedroom window looked out on Potter's House. As a friendly coincidence, she began to offer up that news, but stopped herself short. Suppose Zemmis took pottery classes often, and found out how close her bedroom window was to his school? She sipped her sparkling drink. Zemmis ducked down under the table. When he came up again, he was holding a bowl.

He handed it to Jean. "I made this," he said. The bowl was the color of muddy plums, heavy as a boulder, and large enough to hold the porridge of Mother Bear. It was not beautifully shaped, but neither was it cracked, chipped, or crazed. "How lovely," Jean said.

Jean was admiring the decorative scratchings on Zemmis's bowl when Claude and Edith arrived. They were carrying cocktails they brought from the bar. Jean introduced everybody. Claude and Edith were chatty people, gregarious—yes, very sociable. They promptly engaged Zemmis in vivid descriptions of ceramic pots they had seen on their last trip to Greece. On and on they went about Greek pots. Enough about pots, Jean thought, but there was no stopping them. Luckily, at the microphone, Harriet Marriott was clearing her throat. The reading was about to begin. Jean angled her chair so that her back was turned to Zemmis, and formed a circle that excluded him.

The first group of poems was very long, almost interminable, and Jean sneaked a look at her watch. Edith kicked Jean under the table, and Jean rolled her eyes. Claude took a little nap. Harriet Marriott used endless images of the broken heads and torn-out stuffings of dolls. During the intermission, Claude went to the men's room, Edith went to the ladies' room, and Jean went upstairs to the bar. She brought her martini downstairs to enhance the second set.

During Arthur M. Armlicher's reading, Jean's party was getting hungry, and trying not to yawn. A few tables away, Jean noticed Harriet Marriott making notes on her performance, so she felt comfortable passing napkin notes to Edith like "I'm starving!" and "Tonight's special is grilled tuna!" and "When can we eat?" When Arthur M. Armlicher's last poem, "Death in a Faucet," came to its merciless end, Claude and Edith rushed upstairs to secure a dinner table, while Jean told Harriet Marriott she would call later with her critical opinions, she was too moved to think.

Claude ordered the Two Bruce Lime Chicken, Jean and Edith chose the blackened bluefish. The women also each ordered a glass of white wine, while Claude, who couldn't tolerate more than an ounce of alcohol, asked for iced tea. Relieved as they were that the reading was over, Jean and her friends continued to dwell on the flaws in Harriet Marriott's poems. They were approaching the giggling stage, when Jean felt a presence over her shoulder, and saw Claude's eyebrows shoot up. "Hi, can I join you?" Jean heard Zemmis say. She and Claude spoke simultaneously: Jean said, "We're having a conference," and Claude said, "Sure, pull up a chair." Zemmis listened to Claude.

"Have you ordered yet? What are you having?" he asked, scanning the menu. "How's the chicken in tarragon butter? Is it usually good?" Soon all their attention was focused on him.

Jean burned with annoyance. This was their neighborhood restaurant. The fun of it was not making conversation with strangers, but feeling at home with your friends. Why didn't Zemmis see himself as an intruder? Why did Claude invite him to sit down? Was he being cordial to Zemmis on her behalf, supposing him to be an old chum? How wrong he was, Jean thought, with gritted teeth, as she listened to Zemmis tell Claude and Edith about his positions in lumber, apples, and natural gas. Amazingly, he shared with Claude a near-obsession with old Ronson lighters and stamps. He spoke in strangely formal elocutions, and some sort of clipped foreign accent, like a Third World prince who has conducted a lifetime of diplomacy with Englishmen. At the moment, Zemmis said, he lived way out on the North Shore of Long Island, but had been raised in an orthodox Jewish section of Flushing, New York. Before the next winter, however, he was thinking of moving to Sarasota, Florida, in order to matriculate at the Ringling Brothers and Barnum & Bailey school for clowns.

The waiter took Zemmis's order before clearing the three empty plates. Impulsively, Edith ordered a slice of chocolate mud pie for the rest of them to split for dessert. The dessert arrived before Zemmis's meal. Jean didn't want any. Zemmis helped himself to her share. Watching Zemmis dig into the chocolate pie, Jean wondered if she was having hot flashes. She had started to see stars and to sweat. She announced a trip to the ladies' room. She needed to think.

In privacy, Jean fanned her underarms and splashed cold water on her face. Clown school? Jean wondered how Zemmis managed to afford all his scholarship. She suspected a secret income. She pictured a rabbi, Zemmis's old bearded father, a leader to his people, alone in his temple, crying and keening for Zemmis, his pushy, dysfunctional son. Jean guessed the rabbi would do anything—even send his son to clown school—to keep him from sticking his fork into the hundreds of slices of pie that belonged to the poor trusting members of the rabbi's congregation in Flushing, New York. Jean imagined Zemmis's father arranging a trust fund in a Sarasota bank. She looked in the mirror over the ladies' room sink. Tiny rivulets of washed-away makeup had left a white dot on her nose and fine white stripes on her cheeks.

Jean's gut feeling about Zemmis switched from apprehension to awe. She wasn't sure which intuition was right. She put aside the notion that he was the rabbi's excommunicated son, and considered the possibility that Zemmis was the Messiah himself. Jean didn't know much about theology, but it was certainly the right time of year for the Christ. She put on a fresh coat of makeup. He could also be the excommunicated son of Bonnie and Clyde.

By the time she returned to the table, Zemmis was gone. He faced a long trip to Long Island, Claude said, and didn't want to chance missing the train. Jean squinted at her glass to see if, as a farewell signal, Zemmis had guzzled her wine. "Not to worry, he knows how to reach us," Edith said soothingly. "Claude and I gave him our cards."

Claude and Edith offered to walk Jean to her door. The rain had stopped, leaving a gleaming patina on the previously filthy streets. At home, tiptoing around her sleeping husband, Jean peered out the bedroom window to gauge its distance from Potter's House. She knew it would be stupid from now on to draw open the curtains. But some gesture of good will seemed in order tonight. After rooting around for the right one, Jean put an unlit candle in a goblet and a striped sock filled with catnip on the windowsill. Tomorrow she would install a window gate.

As always, the morning's drama revolved around the melon, last night's honeydew. As soon as Jean cut into it, she knew it was dry. She cut a slice for her husband, who crooned with enjoyment when he tasted it. For a melon that was hard as nails, he said, it was unexpectedly sweet.

from *The Luminosity of Sheets*

3.

While I was living in Greece,
my girlfriend in America had an affair
with a Greek boy, a biology student
named Vassilis, who was renting
a room in the same house as her.

Sweet-tempered, flabby, inexpert,
he made her feel at ease. He was gone
when I got back, but I squeezed
it out of her, all the gory details:
how many times, and what it was like.

The man who owned the house she lived in,
a "special friend" with whom she'd had,
as best as I could make out, no more
than a serious flirtation, was dying
of cancer. By then, the hospitals
wanted nothing to do with him, so
he wasted away at home. Once,
after helping to change his sheets,
she came to me sobbing: "His little penis
was so small. . . ." All that fall,
she was sick with fear about death
and disease—the man didn't want her
around. Neither did I, much.
                                    One day
she hid in his bathroom, scribbling
soul-saving notes to herself. Trying
to muster the courage to face him.
When she came out, he was dead.

We went through a bad spell: the time
she squealed her tires and came
at me in the shopping plaza parking lot.
And the time she flung my Selectric
to the floor: I stared at the pieces,
then turned and punched the wall
instead of her, and cracked a metacarpal.

Just when things were settling down,
word came from Greece: her friend,
Vassilis, had crashed into the back
of a parked farm truck, killing
himself and his Greek fiancée.
She said they must have been fighting
(like us, they were an "old story")
because Vassilis never sped, or drove
recklessly—he wasn't that kind of Greek.

Two years later I was in Athens,
and she asked me to look up his family—
he had a sister in town—and take them
flowers or something. But I don't know,
I couldn't find the name, or no one
answered when I called. Anyway,
I was in a hurry—I had other things
to do, friends of my own to see.

4.

Yesterday, watching the eclipse,
the moon a red clot, I remembered
about those sheets, the ones I stole.
Back in America, I lent them
to Bill, a fellow renting a room
in the same house as me. One night,
in the middle of the night,
boots pounded up the stairs,
someone banged on my door.

It was the cops—four of them.
I directed them to Bill's door.
They arrested him for rape.
Handcuffed him right there, read him
his rights, and led him off.

It was a girl I knew—a friend of sorts.
She'd come by one day when I was out
and hooked up with him.
Nobody knew at the time: not me,
not his girlfriend. It lasted
into winter, then stopped. Then . . .

"I told you about that guy,"
my girlfriend said. "I saw it
in his eyes." They sent him
to the state penitentiary where,
for all I know, he sits to this day,
reading Louis L'Amour novels.
Fantasizing escape.

His two burly brothers moved out his things.
They weren't talking much.
In his closet they found a mountain
of shirts. Things he'd bought and worn
maybe once, or not at all, then tossed
onto the pile. Dozens of them. Go figure.
They carried them down with everything else,
armload after armload. The sheets
must have been buried in there somewhere.

Migrations

Duluth, Minnesota

Read hawk's story ink scrawls
Across   a paper sky   the goodbye
To time
                    A woman
Turning through wrinkled
Leaves
The Wood is in   the Garden
Is in   the Wash
The wind wraps all of us
With winter
                    Almost silence
Then melts ice into spring
Tongues loosen
                    She snaps twigs
Beneath her tie-shoes
On the unpaved road
In her coat is a tomato
From the window sill
The choker chain from the dog
In her coat is all the wilderness
From here to the border
Beating like the heart of a hare
Under the shadow
She is my grandmother
Coming to get me

Her children are the
Wild life
Asleep in the woods
Until my grandfather returns
To the lumber camp
A dump of rusted cans and broken bottles

In his swath
No money   fear
Another conception
She midwifed herself
Made do by selling eggs

The past is north
The past is a fledgling
Inside the Fall
Hawk migration
My grandmother married at sixteen
She told me
Don't get married at sixteen
My grandmother had eleven kids
She said don't have too many
She broke the tether of her body
At the age of eighty-two
In the virgin forest
Where I've come to live

Now   the sky
Wakes to the kettling hawks
I wake to her
To all the emigrants   fierce
Wings
Over the flame
Of leaves

STACEY LAND JOHNSON

Texas and Eternity

I want to talk to ghosts. Where are they in this county.
Over the red grass, under the rancher motels. To freefall
through their gorgeous startling souls, released from time.
My rearview mirror goes dark. I'm not afraid.
Death is the instant of perfected memory.
It seems just like the present tense, just like life,
colorful and quivering. You won't relive your days
but all the things you've imagined. Some people
are saying they're going to heaven. They're imagining heaven.
They're right. The biggest decision is what to work over
in your head and dream about and how much to do it.
A lot of times I don't want to do anything else,
no interruptions, but without what I love in the world
I wouldn't have a reason to imagine. The eternal life
and this one are a braid and it turns to water,
each pours into the other, in the grasp of love.

Communion

I am the tuck of turquoise water,
the slap of spray on ocean rocks.
I am the boat, the effort
of her engines, the voice
of the captain pointing out
the woman whipped against the cliff
by wind, her red cap.
I am the trails of bindweed
at her feet, the labyrinth of roots.
I am the wind that whips
the woman bent to her words.
I am her book of poems and it is I.
I am the pages in it, both written
and blank, the knapsack she drags
behind her like tradition,
her can of cola, her plum.
I am the doe she startles on the path,
the mud mire she skirts,
the stump she stumbles over,
her fall among the stones.
I am the blue door she opens,
the kettle she rinses,
the tea she sips to warm herself.
I am the warm.
I am the purple bruise rising
on her thigh, the salve
she will apply at bedtime.
I am her bed with its shroud
of prickly wool, the bedsprings,
the dust that shapes them like a shadow.
I am the last word she reads
before sleeping and I am her dream

of no words, but of drifting
on a blue/green sea until she
dissolves, then settles like lichen
along the narrow fissures of the rocks.

Postcards

My daughter said she'd found God on a farm in New Mexico. She wrote this on postcards, in the looping handwriting of a child, though she was nineteen and had seen her share of trouble.

"It's not a cult," Laura wrote. "The land is beautiful and the roads are smooth. In the fields there's corn—tiny husks, green and perfect-shaped. God planted them. He built the roads. There's so much I never understood."

"God doesn't build roads," I wrote back. "People do. Mexican workers and kids without college degrees. Come home now and I'll take care of you."

She's my only child. In my room, above the desk, hangs a painting she made for me when she was a girl. I lie in bed at night with my eyes open and try to make out the shape of the painting.

She wasn't alone, she wrote. She had friends who loved her. She had a swami called Ron.

Ron had Ph.D.'s in philosophy and psychology. He'd spent time in Tibet with Buddhist monks and lived in Jerusalem among rabbis. He was, Laura said, a conglomeration of good, a holy man immersed in thought. "Ron's not fly-by-night," she wrote. "At last I'm happy."

I brought her first postcard to Kit Jernigan, the Presbyterian minister who lives next door. He was seated at his desk, reading, shoulders stooped, his red beard dipping toward the pages.

"This isn't good," Kit said.

"What should I do?"

"You can wait. Often they come home after a short while. They get tired and miss their families."

"And if she doesn't?"

"You can try to have her rescued."

"Kidnap her?" I said.

"You can call it that. They rescue these kids and try to deprogram them."

Kit's the closest friend I have in town. Twice a week we go to the gym, where we jog and lift weights, breathe in and out, and soak our shirts, then take a sauna and come home. He has lived in the same house for twenty years. He knew my wife, Ruth, before she got sick; he watched Laura grow up. "She's not a kid," I said.

"I know," said Kit. He put down his reading glasses.

"Are you telling me I should kidnap her?"

"I'm not telling you anything," he said.

I'm fifty-two years old, and have spent a good part of my life alone. I've driven through most of the states in the union, and have lived in six countries and on three different continents. When I was twenty-three I climbed Mount Kilimanjaro; two years ago I walked along the Great Wall of China. In the summer of 1964, I took a bus down south and helped register black voters in Memphis, Tennessee. I've traveled this world and seen its pain, and though I'm a businessman and live comfortably, I do my best to be a good citizen.

I was brought up in the Catholic Church, but I'm no longer religious. I stopped going to confession when I went overseas, and in Munich, in 1962, I drank beer and ate sausage on Good Friday. Now, every few years, I go back to Christmas Mass and just watch. I listen to the voice of the priest, to the gentle rustling of men and women in their pews, clean-scrubbed and reverent on their holy day.

Ruth and I didn't baptize Laura; it seemed hypocritical to do so. But later, after Ruth had died and Laura was in trouble, I wondered about our faithless home, and about the non-believing world we live in—thought maybe if I'd taken Laura to church, pretended I was someone I wasn't, she might have felt rooted and secure, and wouldn't have ended up on a farm two thousand miles from me, hoping to find meaning in her life.

In the attic, I kept a huge stack of books on parenting. *Attachment and Loss; The Making and Breaking of Affectional*

Bonds—more advice than I knew what to do with. I used to read these books at night, in the years following Ruth's death, as if being a parent were a subject I could study, as if the reading itself were protective.

AIDS was in the news. Laura had been staying out late with troubled boys, stringy-haired kids who skulked in the alleyways in scuffed-up cowboy boots, liquor heavy on their breath.

I found Laura in her bedroom when I came home from work. That morning, I'd left her a newspaper article on safe sex. She was fifteen. Already I was corresponding by mail.

She had a large bowl of paste in front of her and was building a pelican out of papier-mâché. "Did you read the article?" I asked.

She pointed to the pile of paper lying on the floor—hundreds of strips of faded newsprint. She dipped her hand into the paste. "The world sucks," she said.

She leaned over her soggy bird. Her legs were pale and hairless, her knees pressed hard against the floor. Around her left ankle was a bracelet of beads; a Tunisian rug, a gift from her mother, hung flat against the wall. A kimono lay carelessly over her wicker chair. It blew in the breeze, casting ribbons across her pale face, my daughter with her kimonos and saris, with her Indian beads, with her James Dean posters and bandannas and SAVE THE RAIN FORESTS buttons. Her patched-up panda lay on the bed, and beside it, on the nightstand, was her diaphragm case. She revered Gandhi and loved Elvis. She was a mishmash of likes and dislikes; and I was her father, fumbling and mute, following her around the house like a ghost, watching her, hoping.

"When you were young," she said, "life was easy. You didn't have to worry about the ozone layer, and no one got shot on the interstates. You did the people you wanted to do."

"Did them?" I said.

"Fucked them. Had sex."

"There were parietals when I was in college," I said. "You got caught in a girl's room and they kicked you out of school. The world was on the brink of disaster. There was the Cuban Missile Crisis and the Bay of Pigs. There was the Vietnam War."

"You didn't fight in Vietnam."

"I lived Vietnam," I said. "The whole country did. No matter what side you were on, it was part of your life."

She leaned over her bowl of paste. "The problem," she said, "is too much information. These scientists are inventing things we never dreamt of—chronic fatigue syndrome, AIDS, I've read about people who sleep seventeen hours a day. What I want to know is why can't there be a disease for people who don't have sex, for grandmothers and Boy Scouts, for instance?"

"Protect yourself," I said. "That's what's important."

She looked at me squarely. "What's the point?"

"You have a full life in front of you. I want it to be healthy and happy." I reached out and took her hand; her fingers were bony and vulnerable. "If you died, I'd be alone in this world. I'd have absolutely nothing to live for."

She looked up at me, and for an instant her face softened, and in her eyes I saw the weight of my needing her, of my asking her to be happy for me.

She pulled her hand away. "Something will kill me in the end. I just read about this guy who had part of his stomach removed. He'd been eating sushi, chic Japanese place, everyone sitting barefoot on those pillows? There were worms in his mackerel. You can't even eat fish anymore."

"You can eat fish," I said. "You just have to cook it. It's like meat, you don't eat raw meat."

"Some people do. There's this tribe in North Africa that subsists on nothing but raw lion's meat. They're tall and muscular, and they all live until they're a hundred and twenty."

"You have an answer for everything," I said.

"What's that supposed to mean?"

I leaned toward her. "It means I care about you. It means I want to make sure you're all right."

"I'm fine," she said. "Everything's fine. Everyone and everything. Hunky-dory. Got it?"

Her mother had died the previous November, a month before Thanksgiving. We'd planned to have dinner in the hospital, to bring turkey, and yams with marshmallows, and eat by Ruth's bed.

This is what she hoped for, my wife with her insides torched out. She wanted to watch us eat.

"I hate Thanksgiving," Laura said. It was the two of us now, and I'd burnt the turkey. I wore a brown tweed jacket and a tie, as if we had company, as if this were a date. In the silver hoops of Laura's earrings, I could see the reflection of cranberries.

"It's a disgusting holiday," Laura said. "We ripped off the Indians." As a child, she'd played Pocohontas in the school play. She'd brought home husks of corn and painted the kernels red and orange, planting them in the garden, hoping to grow maize. "Manhattan for twenty-four dollars. I can't believe it."

I flipped over the turkey wing so it wouldn't look burnt.

"You're supposed to baste it," she said. "It keeps the bird moist." She laid her palms along the rim of her plate. "You're more than three times as old as I am, so why do I have to teach you these things?"

"Please, sweetie. I don't want us to fight."

She stared at the bird, splayed out on its back like a baby.

"Your turkey's getting cold," I said.

"I'm a vegetarian now."

"What's that supposed to mean?"

"I've decided this instant to become a vegetarian."

"You can't just decide. I wanted us to eat together, for everything to be perfect."

"Well, everything's not perfect," she said. "Nothing is." She pointed her fork at the turkey. "They killed that thing. They killed it just like they killed Mom."

"No one killed Mom."

"They radiated her to death. They yanked out her hair and shot her into the sky, turned her into a fucking reactor."

When I looked up, she was crying. "Sweetie," I said, and reached out to touch her. Her shoulders were hunched over and her chest heaved.

"What am I going to do?" she said. "It's just me now—me and this big world out there."

"I'm here. We have each other."

She pinched her arm. "Look at me, I'm starting to grow fat."

"You're beautiful," I said.

"Would you think that if you were my age? If you were a guy in my high school, would you even bother talking to me?"

"I'd love you, young or old," I said.

She looked up at me. Big tears the color of her earrings dripped down toward the edge of her plate. "Oh God," she said, "I'm such a fucking burden. I love you, you know, and here I am ruining your Thanksgiving dinner—like you bargained for this, like you thought you'd ever have to bring me up alone, me taking over your life."

"You *are* my life," I said. "You're the only thing that matters to me anymore."

She left home the first time when she was seventeen. I'd agreed she could be on her own if she finished high school. She graduated, barely, and skipped commencement. A week later she drove cross-country in a pink polka-dotted van, then spent a year in Boise, Idaho, where she raised horses for a man she'd met at a Denny's. He drove a Kawasaki, and had been sitting in the booth next to hers, smoking cigarettes and dropping the ashes by her feet.

"His name is Axel," Laura said. She was calling from a pay phone along Route 84. "Could you send me my tapes?"

"What does he do?" I asked.

"He owns horses." Beyond her, through the static, I could hear the sounds of tires screeching.

"Do you know him?"

"Sort of. I do now."

"He could kill you," I said.

"Anyone can. I heard about this man who shot his wife and kids. Rich guy—jacket and tie, the whole bit. Came home one night and just blew them away."

"His name is Axel?"

"Dad," she said, but then her change ran out.

It was the fall of 1990, and the country was preparing for war. You could see it in the polls, and on the faces of the newscasters and the people in government. Laura had left an address where I could reach her, and I sent her messages on the back of postcards.

"Our soldiers will be fighting in the Middle East," I wrote. "What do you think of that?"

"Send money," she wrote back.

I thought it over. I could try to starve her and make her come home. But who knew where she might end up, my daughter with nothing but a tattered duffel bag and a horse breeder she'd met on the side of the highway. I phoned Kit and asked him for advice. Then I wired her five hundred dollars.

Now, with Laura on the farm, I drove to the city, to a huge postcard warehouse on Bleecker Street. I found Ansel Adams photos, and cards with Rembrandts painted on them. There were New Age postcards; crystals in dizzying patterns; holograms; black-and-white snapshots from the Thirties and Forties; Slavic men in fur hats standing by pickle stands.

I bought Laura postcards of horses—sleek stallions, Arabian mares, Stevie Cauthen riding Secretariat, a photo finish at the Belmont Stakes. I'd taken Laura riding when she was little.

"Wild horses," I wrote, drawing the words carefully in felt-tip pen. "Wild horses couldn't drag me away / Wild, wild horses we'll find them someday."

"Why are you sending me these notes?" she wrote back. This was a pictureless card, bought with a stamp already printed on it. "That's not a father-daughter song, it's a song for lovers. Besides, I don't like the Stones anymore, they do nothing for me. P.S.," she wrote, "it's 'ride them'—'We'll ride them someday.' You got the lyrics wrong."

I sent her a card with Miss Piggy on the front. Miss Piggy was holding a briefcase and wearing curlers and yellow sunglasses. She looked like Liz Smith. "Mike Tyson squeezed all eight of my teats," Miss Piggy said. "Clarence Thomas stole my panties, and it'll cost big bucks for me to tell what happened at the Kennedy compound."

"Look what's happening in our country," I wrote. "Awful people are being appointed to the Court. You're isolated, Laura. There's a big crazy world crying out for your help and you're ignoring it."

"I'm ignoring what's worth ignoring," she wrote back. "Ron's the only thing that matters and I'm not ignoring him. We love each other here—we love Ron and he loves us—what more does the world need? If you cared about me, Daddy, if you loved me, you'd want to know how I was doing, you wouldn't be writing me about politics."

"Of course I love you," I wrote. "Tell me anything, darling. I just want some correspondence between us, I want to know what's on your mind and in your heart."

"Ron's in my heart," she wrote. "He makes me happy—happier than any man ever has or ever will."

Once, before she could talk, when she was tiny and fig-like, I couldn't imagine her having an opinion. She'd learn words and sentences. But a mind of her own. She grew bigger—slow, imperceptible—until she was gangly and pubescent, until she was who she was, and I tried to pinpoint the moment she stopped needing me, the moment she so much didn't need me I wondered if she ever did.

She got chicken pox and strep throat. I worried about rheumatic fever. She sneaked candy and soda into the house. She hid Tootsie Roll lollipops under her mattress. Her arteries were filled with cholesterol; sugar ran through them, and Red Dye #2. She drank too much beer and wrecked a car. A bong sat on her bureau, a turquoise bong in the shape of a woman's body. She asked me to grow pot in our garden. "We can control what's in it," she said. "Who knows what's in the stuff I buy on the streets."

At night, when she was out, I listened for the sound of sirens. I waited up to hear a key. I asked her what she did with her friends, wanting to know what I shouldn't have wanted to know, because knowing only made me stay up longer.

I thought about nature versus nurture. I wondered which one let me off the hook.

I had slapped her once, a quick angry stroke across the face. Again I wondered—wondered if that was the reason she went wrong, if finally I could blame myself.

These are the questions I asked: How much television? What kind of food? Should I help her with her homework or hope she perseveres? The day she was born, Ruth and I opened a bank account in her name. We added cash every year, so someday she could pay for college. When she left home at seventeen, I refused to give her the money. "Come back," I said, "and go to college." A year later, when she was in Boise, I suggested junior college. She was raising horses with a man I'd never met, and junior college sounded good to me. Now I didn't care about college. I offered her bribes on the back of postcards. "The money is yours," I wrote. "Come home and get it, use it as you like. Use your own bad judgment."

That day, on the way back from the postcard warehouse, I saw a retarded girl along the New Jersey Turnpike. She was about four, and she stood with her parents at a rest stop. The girl's face was slack and puffy, her head angled to the side, her gait was uncertain. Down's Syndrome, I thought. I looked away.

This is what you fear. You decide to have a baby. You take care of yourself, you eat the proper food, you pray for the right number of chromosomes. But as I looked back at that child, chubby-fingered and helpless, a girl who'd grow older but would never leave home, for a foolish instant I regretted my life and wished I could switch places with her parents.

For a time I thought Laura would be an artist. Ruth painted, as did her mother before her, and I myself keep a sketchbook. I sit in the garden when the afternoon is warm and draw what I see.

In Laura's painting, the one that hangs above my desk, a man and a monkey are sitting at an ice cream parlor eating banana splits. The monkey holds a spoon in his hand. Around his neck hangs a bib. Laura painted the picture when she was seven. For three months it hung on the wall of a Howard Johnson's next to the art of other schoolchildren. These are the words of a parent, I know, but when I look at that painting, at the expressiveness drawn on the monkey's face, I'm convinced this is the work of a sensitive soul.

I hadn't heard from Laura in three weeks, so I called Kit and got the name of a deprogrammer.

"Have you met him?" I asked.

"No," he said, "but I'm told he does good work."

I drove to the man's house wearing a pin-striped suit and black loafers; I'd gotten a haircut earlier that day. I wondered who usually came for this man's help: divorced parents, alcoholics, fathers and mothers in unkempt clothing. He'd ask me questions, want details about my life. Already I resented him.

He was no more than thirty, and had a full head of auburn hair. His skin was pearly and unwrinkled; he sported sideburns. How, I wondered, had he gotten into this business? Did he know someone like Laura? A girlfriend? A brother or sister who'd been lured away? Maybe he enjoyed other people's trauma; here was someone who loved a chase.

He had his diploma on the wall—Haverford, a good college.

"Mr. Williamson," I said.

"Call me Ralph."

Ralph. Ron. Everyone had a name like that.

"So," said Ralph. There was crumpled newspaper on the floor. An empty coffee cup, its handle chipped, lay on its side by the carpet. A few feet away sat a soggy tea bag. To my right, three tube socks hung on the spine of a rattan chair. None of them matched. Maybe Ralph was disorganized, maybe he forgot details. He stared at me coolly, his palms folded on his lap. "Where exactly is your daughter?"

"In New Mexico," I said.

"It's a big state. We'll need to locate her." He laid his hands along the edge of the sofa. They were large hands, pink and fleshy, athletic, the hands of a fighter. "This will cost you, Lawrence. I hope you understand."

I looked up. I hadn't asked him to call me by my first name.

"One thing you should know," he said. "Sometimes the subject doesn't come voluntarily."

"The subject?" I said.

"In this case your daughter."

"You mean you'll have to rough her up?"

"We try our darndest not to do that, Lawrence. Do you remember Carter and the Iranian hostages? They botched the rescue, the helicopters didn't even get off the ground. On the other hand, there was Entebbe. Entebbe was perfect."

"Entebbe wasn't perfect," I said. "A passenger died in the hospital, and an Israeli soldier was shot to death."

"They were in Uganda," Ralph said. "Try rescuing someone from Uganda."

"We're not in Uganda," I said. "We're here, in Bergen County. What does Uganda have to do with it? This is my daughter and no terrorists are involved. No guns either, I hope."

Ralph looked at me smugly. "I was just trying to make a comparison."

At the gym the next day, Kit pumped me with questions.

"I didn't like him," I said.

"You don't have to like him. You just have to trust he'll do his job."

We were on the track, running abreast. Kit lived alone, he'd never been married or had children. He cared about Laura, but I was her father. He could manage to be happy without seeing her again.

"Sleep on it a while, then trust your instincts."

"What would you do?"

"It's not up to me."

"Give me a straight answer," I said.

"I don't have a straight answer," said Kit.

"I'm having Ron's baby," Laura wrote the next week. "He's my husband and father, we're populating the world with his children. We're starting a genetic revolution—soon all the women will give birth. Someday you'll meet him, Dad, and then you'll understand."

"I don't want to meet Ron," I wrote back. "He's not your father. He's a hoodlum and a crook. What do you mean you're having his baby? I should call the cops. You girls are concubines, all of you."

I crumpled the letter and started again.

> Dear Laura,
>
> I'm very sick. The doctor says I have six months to live. I must see you at once.
>
> Love,
> Dad

"I can't visit you," she wrote back. "Ron has forbidden it. But if you're well enough, you can fly to Albuquerque and meet me at the airport. Ron will give us some time together. He's a wonderful, compassionate man."

Wonderful. Compassionate. I booked a flight for the following week.

Laura was waiting at the gate when I arrived. I stepped forward gingerly and placed my bag by my feet; then I took hold of her in my arms.

"Daddy," she said.

"Your voice," I said, "it's beautiful."

She took a step back. Her blond hair had been cropped short; she looked like a tomboy. Her biceps had thickened, her veins shone through. I quickly scanned her body. She seemed healthy. There were no bruises, none that I could see. "Dad," she said, "this is Ron."

A man about forty stuck out his hand; I'd thought she would come alone.

Ron was a philosopher and psychologist, according to Laura, but to me he looked like a high school gym coach. He was sandy-haired and had a small button nose and a firmly set jaw. His skin was creased and leathery, with a slightly orange, artificial hue, as if he'd spent too much time in a tanning salon. He was about six foot three and had a short tree stump of a neck. His Adam's apple bobbed in his throat.

I'd expected something different. Moses, the Dalai Lama, flowing cape, high forehead, braided hair, furrowed brow. Ron stood opposite me with his hands behind his back. My daughter worshipped a football player.

"I need time with you alone," I said.

"We'll have to ask Ron's permission."

"Thug," I muttered.

"What?" said Laura.

Ron hesitated for a moment. "You have fifteen minutes," he said.

We went across the terminal, to a darkened lounge with sofa seats, a cross between a restaurant and bar. It was called Prey and Potion, and it looked like an indoor game park, with furs and pelts along the walls, and a long bar with rifles dangling from the ceiling, and a bartender who wore a black leather cowboy hat and boots and spurs. A moose head hung from the wall above us.

"I thought you were coming by yourself," I said.

"Ron and I are inseparable. Even when I'm far away, he's still with me."

"Sounds like a disease," I said.

"Here," Laura said, "feel my stomach." She grabbed hold of my hand and pressed it against her. "Soon the baby will be kicking. It's incredible, there's been no morning sickness." She hesitated for a moment. "I hope you're alive when it's born. I want you to be a grandpa."

"I'll be alive," I said. "Nothing's wrong with me."

The waiter strutted toward us, crossing a row of rugs, one animal pelt after another. Dark tattoos covered both his forearms.

"What's on tap?" I asked.

Laura raised her hand to stop me. "I don't drink," she said.

I looked up at the waiter. "We'll have tea."

"There's Chamomile, Sleepy Time, Celestial Seasonings, Red Zinger—"

"Tea," I said, "plain tea."

"O.K., buster." He tipped his cowboy hat and walked off.

In the back of the lounge two men were playing pinball. *Rodeo Ripper,* read the neon sign, and I could see purple lights flashing and hear the sound of bells and sirens and automated voices shouting, *Lasso him, cowboy, kick his butt.*

I turned toward Laura. "I want you to come home. We can take care of the pregnancy and forget it ever happened. I'll send you to art school if you'd like. You used to paint, you know. I still have your artwork on my wall."

"Take care of the pregnancy? I'm an adult now, remember that." She turned toward the entrance, where Ron watched over us like a sentinel. The moose head stared down from the wall.

"Do you remember when you were little and we had tea parties in the garden? You, me, and Mom?"

"I pray for you constantly," Laura said. "We all do."

"Listen to me," I told her, "we'll go back east this evening, I've already bought two tickets."

"I'm staying here," she said. "I'm the happiest I've been in my whole life." She dipped her spoon into the tea.

"How would Mom feel about this? What would she think if she were still alive?"

"She's not alive," Laura said. "Who cares about Mom?"

"I do. I think about you both all the time. If you come back with me, you can stay home and rest a while and I'll take care of you. Then you can go to college."

"I'm not going to college," she said, "because college won't make me happy. Don't you want me to be happy, Dad?"

"Of course," I said, but when I looked up she was crying.

"No you don't," she blurted.

And as I watched her sob, I knew she was right, knew I'd grown old, too lonely to listen for fear I might lose her, only I'd lost her already, she wasn't mine. I did my best, I wanted to say, but the words wouldn't come. I reached out to touch her, but I grabbed too hard, and in a flash Ron was over, tugging on her in the other direction. There was a frenzy of grunts, not a word was exchanged, just Ron and me pulling on Laura's arms. Her biceps bulged, her face was contorted; with Ron's help she pushed me against the back of my chair. "Laura, sweetheart!" I cried. I tried to take hold of her, but she was out of reach. She grabbed Ron's hand and ran off.

I tried to compose myself. Tea had spilled across the tablecloth and onto my trousers. My underwear was wet. I closed my eyes, and for the first time in thirty years I began to pray. "Help me," I murmured, to a God I didn't recognize and couldn't believe in. I opened my eyes. The waiter was standing across from me, and in the background I could hear the automated voices of the pinball machine shouting on. I continued to pray, but I wasn't sure what to ask for, and at that moment I knew I'd become like Laura— grown closer to her than ever before, cast off and looking for something. I looked down at the table and could see my reflection in the open mouth of my teaspoon: sweaty, pepper-haired, and upside down.

I paid my bill and stepped out into the terminal. For a second, I thought I saw Laura. It was another girl, walking with an older man—her father, her boyfriend, I couldn't tell what. She stood on tiptoe and whispered in his ear; he touched the lace edge of her collar. They walked across the terminal and got onto the escalator. Then they rose out of sight.

My Spiritual Advisor

"She propped her false leg up in the corner…"

my spiritual advisor says when a strong man comes
into the room you flutter your eyelashes & hike
up your skirts
when a strong man commands your heart flutters
skips a beat and you do as you wish ghandi and dr king
called it passive resistance i would call it the iron
hard way of the nordic gypsy queens

my spiritual advisor has given up on me
again it's not unusual
for me to ask a question over and over again
when i don't like the answer

fool he says things are a mess one is confused
he says weak stubborn sick
someone among enemies someone
is being talked about

you
he says you are joyful
joyful

i'm beginning to think i have problems
yes he says discipline is called for
passion obscures
beauty can't decide
anything serious

i'm beginning to think he's too old
to be taken seriously
he says don't be impatient let things
develop
slowly
and
quietly
he says something about a kind of bird that never mates
again
he goes on and on

i'm getting confused and can hardly hear him anymore
why did i ever think he could help me
i need a good rest
more than any holy man
you
tempting as a credit card
and no strong men left standing

An Ordinary Woman

an ordinary woman leaves her body here
when she's done with it
a litterbug
she leaves a burden and a warning to us
but the dancer's body is completely gone
aah!
a jitterbug
her soul remains here with us
an encouragement
what are we supposed to do with it

JAMES SCOFIELD

The Housekeeper

My father loved her, or rather, wanted her.
Gaudy and baubled, with long nut-brown legs,
and sun-blazed hair; yes, he wanted her, bad,
and the bitch knew it. She was twenty-five, he
was fifty-two, I was eleven, mother was dead.
The night it happened she was drunk, dinner
was over, the dishes were catching flies,
and she was outside, sitting with some sailor
in a new Chevy. I remember my father
and me on the couch, watching Hawkeye cut up
Frank Burns, and Father not laughing.
He scratched a two-day-old stubble, then dropped
his big hands onto bony knees—he was tired,
nervous, his eyes twitching, glancing at the door.
Suddenly a man howled in pain, and a minute
later she stormed through the kitchen door,
naked from the waist down to her painted toes.
Up she went onto those toes, and danced over
to my father, then twirling her cotton panties
above her head, she did a clumsy pirouette
disappearing into her bedroom slamming the door.
Soon the boyfriend staggered into the kitchen
and followed her through that door. My father
got up, his fists clenched, and went off to bed.

I waited. Two hours. Then, I cracked her door;
the sailor coughed, turned over, then snored.
Still awake she smiled, her hand moved, waving me in.
I sat on the floor, with one finger she made ringlets
in my hair, then moved her hand down my chest.
Slowly she lifted me up, and soon I lay
between her and the sailor; the light went out.

She pulled my head close, moved her tongue across
my lips, slipped it into my mouth and out.
I found her breasts; small, firm, and damp. My hand,
moved down, she grabbed it, then slowly relented.
I tried to leave, but the sailor rolled over
and I was stuck between them! "Lucky,
you pig, get over!" she yelled. Lucky snorted,
an arm moved, and I was free. In the early light
I saw a tattoo: "Lucky loves Lucky,"
and one eye open, staring—I froze; and he snored.

I lay in bed, my hands behind my head.
I jumped as the alarm went off, hoarse and rough.
Slowly my father reached, turning it off.
I turned and saw his eyes staring at the ceiling.
Finally he got up, and sat with his feet
on the floor, holding his head in his hands.
It was four o'clock in the morning. He looked
around at his children, seven in one room,
slowly reached for his boots and dressed for work.

The Slaughter

1.

Everything we ate was on foot. We didn't have
the Norge or the Frigidaire, only salt to keep.
Autumn's hog went in brine for days,
swimming. You had to boil forever
just to get the taste out. I loved winter
& its chitlins, but boy I hated cleaning.
If not from the hogs, we got fresh bucketsful
from our slaughterhouse kin. White folks
got first pick, even of guts. They loved

that stuff, but to us it was only a season, just
making do. Home, you cut innards in strips,
put water in one end, held the other tight
then seesawed them back & forth. Afterwards
we dumped the excess in a hole dug out
back. I always make sure folks clean them
a second time. Don't eat chitlins
at just anyone's filthy old house.

2.

Chickens went like dusk. Before
twilight, Mama said go get me a hen
& me in that swept yard, swinging one round
by the neck, the pop, then dropping it.
We wrung, but some folks chopped, the chicken
flapping awhile before it fell, headless, a sight.
Feathers we plucked told us that soon
cold would come indoors like greens after

first frost. Everything then tasted so different
& fresh, a sister's backtalk, but I wouldn't want
back those days for all the known world.
No sir. Some nights dinner would just get up
& run off cause I hadn't wrung it right,
others we'd eat roosters tougher
& older than we were, meat so rough Mama
couldn't cut it with her brown, brown eyes.

The Preserving

Summers meant peeling: peaches,
pears, July, all carved up. August
was a tomato dropped
in boiling water, my skin coming
right off. And peas, Lord,
after shelling all summer, if I never
saw those green fingers again
it would be too soon. We'd also
make wine, gather up those peach
scraps, put them in jars & let them
turn. Trick was enough air.

Eating something boiled each meal,
my hair in coils by June first, Mama
could barely reel me in from the red
clay long enough to wrap my hair
with string. So tight
I couldn't think. But that was far
easier to take care of, lasted all
summer like ashy knees.
One Thanksgiving, while saying grace
we heard what sounded like a gunshot
ran to the back porch to see
peach glass everywhere. Someone
didn't give the jar enough room

to breathe. Only good thing
bout them saving days was knowing
they'd be over, that by Christmas
afternoons turned to cakes: coconut
yesterday, fruitcake today, fresh
cushaw pie to start tomorrow.
On Jesus' Day we'd go house
to house tasting each family's peach

brandy. You know you could stand
only so much, a taste. Time we weaved
back, it had grown cold as war.
Huddling home, clutching each
other in our handed down hand-
me-downs, we felt we was dying
like a late fire; we prayed
those homemade spirits
would warm most way home.

Blackberries

Yesterday I fell into a ditch
trying to reach across
to the fattest prizes—slipped,
my rump hitting the prickly ground
so hard I thought of sudden love.

The ripest ones
will drop into your hand
at a brush of the branch.
I can spot them now, the ones
so black they're almost blue,
crow-colored. That ready,
they don't cling to their caps,
but wish themselves into the air,
onto the tongue.

I'm not even put off by the spiders
I hate. I blow, and they
dissolve into leaves.

Today my right hand still burns
from the nettles. The skin seems
to be buzzing—first above the wrist,
then below it, following the pulse.
It makes me dream of blackberries.
I tell you, they ache for pastry
to hold them, for the mouth
I put now to my humming hand.

Lasting

*When the first radio wave music escaped Earth's ionosphere, it
literally did become eternal. Music, in this century, has been
converted from sound into the clarity of pure light.
Radio has superseded the constraints of space.*
—Leonard Shlain, *Art & Physics*

Imagine Vivaldi suddenly falling
on the ears of a woman
somewhere beyond Alpha Centauri,
her planet spun into luminescence
aeons from now. She might be
much like us, meditating
on the body, her lover murmuring
to the underside of her breast
before its heaviness suspends,
for a moment, the lift and pause
of his breath. A music she almost knows
drifts through centuries, startling,
augmenting her pleasure.
When earth is particles of dust,
Orson Welles may still strike fear
into the hearts of millions
who wake one morning, unaware
that light has arrived
as an audible prank. Ezra Pound might rasp
his particular madness from an Italy
still alive in arias that shower
into the open windows
of a world youthful as hope.
When books are no longer even ashes,
and no heart beats in any space
near where we were, suns
may intersect, and some of our voices
blend into choirs, the music of the spheres
adrift among new stars.

from Him

R honda felt Cy's ribs through his T-shirt that proclaimed
ROCK-AND-ROLL in thunderbolt letters. The leather jacket he
wore today magnified him: his height, the breadth of his shoulders, the glimmer of fear he struck in her. Suddenly she was afraid
that this was all they had, a striking look that turned heads, a few
sexy poses in bed, and nothing whatever to say to each other. Cy
kissed her in a quick greeting.

"Stuff," he said. "You're my stuff."

She smiled. "What is *that*?"

"A ghetto term. You like that, huh?"

"Yes."

His smell of leather and soap, the pressure of his arm around
her, and most of all his rich voice felt like a breath of oxygen on
an alien planet. He took her hand, and they headed toward Sixth
Avenue. She made things too difficult. Cy worried about being
hungry, as usual, and where to find the nearest Blimpie's. She
pretended to search with him, but her mind hummed along on
its own track in spite of her, fretful, preparing for loss.

As Cy tugged at Rhonda's hand, rushing her along toward the
train, she remembered something she hadn't thought of in years.
Another sunny afternoon in Wichita, when she was ten, when
someone had taken her hand and pulled her in.

Her father had taken her visiting, as he often did on Sundays
after the morning service. The deacons gathered in a room at the
church to be assigned cards with names and addresses of people
who'd visited once on a special occasion, or of members who
hadn't come in a month of Sundays. Sometimes they simply went
from door to door in the church's neighborhood, a mostly poor
area in central Wichita. Most of the members lived on the
wealthier edges of the city. The deacons went calling to let the
stray sheep know they'd been missed, to deliver the holiday food

baskets, and to take inventory of immediate needs. Hospital visits and invalids were assigned to Wednesday nights; one Saturday a month they did yard work for the elderly.

Her father didn't ask her to come with him on the hospital and yard-work visits. Another deacon went then. But when he had to go ask people why they hadn't been to church and if they were saved, Rhonda had to come along, still in her church dress. She sat and listened to the adults. She liked their conversations, but when she joined in, they laughed. She didn't like her father to tell how good her grades were, and how proud he and her mother were. Everyone looked at her as if she were odd, not unique. And once he'd started in about her, she knew that if there was a piano in the house, she would have to play some hymns.

Hymns, of course. She knew most of them would rather hear a popular song, something they'd recognize from the radio, but she didn't know those songs. Only hymns.

That day they'd gone in the car because the address was too far north to walk, up in the black part of town. Her father parked in the sun to avoid the big dying elms. She wasn't sure if the trees themselves dropped the stuff on your hood that ate away the paint or if the birds did. The car in front of them had a smashed back windshield, a circular webbed break that glittered fiercely. Rhonda closed her eyes, but she could still see it on her eyelids, burned in reverse.

Her father looked at the house two doors down, a crackerbox duplex like most of its neighbors. A group of children played list-lessly on the hard-packed dirt yard, mercilessly sunbaked except for the two steps leading to the door. Only the screen, ripped out of its frame at one corner, separated them from the dark mystery inside.

"Come on, then," her father said. "There's nothing to be afraid of. They're people, just like us."

Rhonda wasn't so sure of how alike they were. Their clothes were old with spots or tears, the kind her mother would throw away or show her how to mend. Their new clothes were too bright, of flashy thin store-bought material. And nobody in her neighborhood took a notion to paint their house pink or purple. She knew her house wasn't as fancy as a lot of others, but they had a tire swing, and forsythia and lilac bushes that her grand-mother had planted on either side of the front door. Here no-body seemed to care what their yards looked like—or hers, either.

Her father walked slowly up the sidewalk while all the children followed him with their eyes.

"Hi, y'all," he said. He talked more country when trying to make friends. "We're from Immanuel Baptist. The church? Your mama at home?"

The mother appeared in the doorway then, her eyes only a shade lighter than the darkness behind her. She pulled down the front of her lime cotton tank over her shorts.

"I'm their mama. You from the school?"

"No, ma'am. We're from Immanuel Baptist Church. Says here on this visitor's card that Antoinette and Roy came to Sunday school a couple months ago. We like to stop by after somebody visits and say howdy."

"Oh, them kids," she said wearily. "They shouldn'ta filled out no cards. I told 'em, go one time on that bus, then that's it. Eat all the doughnuts you can hold, then you go back to reg'lar church with the rest of us."

"Doughnuts?" her father said. He pressed his lips together, then he gave up and smiled. Gravely, he said, "I see. So you all have your membership placed in another fellowship."

At that moment a girl smaller than Rhonda appeared quietly next to her. Her dark cheeks pushed up her oval blue glasses when she smiled. She squinted to keep them in place.

"Let's play," she said. She took Rhonda's hand matter-of-factly and led her away to the backyard.

Rhonda couldn't remember the girl's name or what they'd actually played. What remained was the feeling when the girl had taken her hand and drawn her in, unquestioningly, not deciding over cruel weeks whether she wanted to be Rhonda's friend. At the same time she remembered how happy she'd been when her father finally called her back to the porch and said they'd been invited to the evening church.

Rhonda and Cy got off the Q train in Brooklyn at Parkside Avenue, an exposed station near Prospect Park, and came out onto a wide street busy with blacks. Cy let go of her hand as they left the subway station.

"A lot of people know me around here," he said. "I don't want her to hear something."

They waited at the corner of Flatbush and Parkside for the light. A car drove by, its speakers booming bass in hypnotic rhythm. Like Brighton Beach, the buildings were mostly two and three stories, but this street was as lively as the Brighton ones were dead. Here everybody was outside in the cool fall day, picking through bins of Caribbean roots and vegetables, looking in store windows at gold chains and earrings, or searching tables piled with rubber shoes. A gaggle of uniformed schoolgirls thronged an open-air pizza shop on the corner.

They crossed when the traffic was close to clear, Cy's usual jump of the gun. On Clarkson they turned off and the street grew quieter and more residential.

"Quite a neighborhood," Rhonda said.

"All kinda niggers," he said. "We got the Jamaicans, the Dominicans. The ones born here. I don't know where the fuck they all come from. And they all hate each other." He laughed dryly. A block later he slowed in front of a large apartment building. "Cloak and dagger time," he said. "Walk a little ways behind me, O.K.? Sometimes the landlady's out in the hallway. She's got to check everybody out."

They met no one, though. Cy led the way to an apartment at the back of the building on the ground floor and opened the door.

Inside, a double mattress neatly made with burgundy sheets took up most of the living-room floor. No room for a couch or easy chair, a bean bag sat in one dusty corner, a small television in the corner closest to the bed. To the right was an eating space—half a room, really part of the kitchen.

No one had troubled to clean for a very long time. The dirt had worn away in paths, but the corners were furry with dust. On the far side of the mattress, Rhonda noticed a pair of shoes, electric blue flats stretched wide, the pointy toes scuffed to white. She pictured a tired black woman with fat feet, the cleaning woman too beat to care for her own.

"That's where you'll find me, every night," Cy said. He nodded at the TV and hunched his shoulders. "On the bed, like this, watching my shows. And she's in there at the table, pecking away, practicing."

A typewriter surrounded by a litter of papers covered the dining table. The cleaning woman aspired to secretarial heights.

"You're not here *every* night," Rhonda said.

"That reminds me." He put the chain on the door and took off his shirt.

August hot that night, and no notion of air conditioning. Paper fans took the place of hymn books in the pew backs, cardboard advertisements for some defunct funeral home, reminders to get right with the Lord now. The only whites in a full black church, Rhonda had wondered if her family was their first. It seemed impossible now, crazy, but when she was ten years old, she'd believed it.

"Where's the ones you talked to?" her mother had whispered when the piano player started up, no music book on the stand.

"I don't see them," her father had said quietly. "Maybe they're late."

"Maybe they think this is funny," her mother hissed. "Something might happen to the *car* out there. Did you think about that?"

"It will be all right," her father said sternly over her sisters' heads. They huddled together, their usual civil war tamed into peace.

Rhonda was the last into the pew, after her father. She wanted to see everything, though she shrank back at first when the choir sang out from the back of the church. They didn't blend together like the singers at Immanuel. As they marched down the aisle and filed into the pews on the stage, Rhonda could pick out each voice as she looked at them. One dark woman sang with a hard brassy edge; another yellowish man couldn't resist adding a little dip to every other note.

The choir blared through two songs without pausing, then the director faced the congregation and raised his hands. Everyone stood, Rhonda's family scrambling up a few moments late, and began a hymn she didn't know. *It's me, it's me, O Lord, standin' in the need of prayer.*

"Come down, Jesus!" a woman said behind them.

A husky man in a white shirt and black tie took the two steps onto the podium in a leap. A Bible raised in one hand, he prayed for a long time while the choir hummed and the piano got slower and softer. The preacher started quietly, then his voice grew louder, gaining power like a pipe organ. He shook the Bible at the ceiling with each new phrase, the people's *amen*s dropped into the short silent gaps.

"Red is definitely your color," Cy said. He crouched over her, still in his underwear. He pushed her knees open with his own, then sat back on his heels for a moment and ran both hands up the outsides of her thighs. "I can't believe how you *look*," he said, and gave one of his shivers. "*Jesus.*"

"Come here," she said.

"Yes, Jesus," her father said once, quietly. Rhonda looked at him. His head was bowed and his eyes squinted closed, his fingers laced together, fighting each other. Her eyes met her mother's in the space in front of him.

"Create in me a clean heart, O God!" the preacher shouted, and a chorus of agreement rose around them. The piano player dived on the keys in a new burst, the choir director's arms swung up, and the singers all yelled at once. The preacher opened his arms to embrace them, his white palm and splayed fingers facing them on one side, the worn black Bible pressed into a deep indentation under his other thumb. The congregation stood and began to file to the front, singing.

I wanted to go down front, thought Rhonda as she lay sprawled in the middle of the wine-red sheets. She lifted her head and freed her hair. *I wanted to go down to the altar with them, but I didn't. My mother was watching.*

High above her, Cy lifted her by her knees and came down hard until she thought she would never be whole again, his hard thighs and his forearms always a part of her, his dark body all she could see. Her heart beat three times, or thirty, and she heard him come, almost shouting.

A woman on the back row of the choir raised her hands and gave a shout toward heaven. The music never stopped pleading, and she stood, her hands raised, and screamed. Her fingers trembled and wavered faster as her voice rose in terror, begging for mercy. Finally she ran from the church through a door at the side, painted white to blend in. It seemed at first she'd burst through the wall. No one followed.

"Did I hurt you, baby?" Cy said.

"A little."

He kissed her and she smiled. She loved to touch his arms.

"I won't do that again," he said.

As a key turned in the lock and the door hit the end of the chain, it struck her that he might be right.

What Difference Does It Make?

When the giant panda views another
of her species through a window, in a mirror,
does she feel a little less lonely?
I smile when I see another couple like us,
though of course they aren't like us,
except for the contrast
between white skin, and black.

The year I turned twelve
the way we live was still a crime.
Loving vs. Virginia made race irrelevant
in marriage, told Richard and Mildred they could live
where they were born.

I thought it nothing to write about,
only one kind of difference in a world of difference,
not at all the most important thing about us,
no shame and nothing to brandish like a badge.
I thought that what should not matter, did not.

Others see *an odd couple,*
all she could get, a trophy, a burden.
Has he bought my whiteness with his maleness?
Or does his blackness accompany my womanhood
in the same swampy place?

Through his eyes I see the pain
of interviews that go well on the phone,
the patronage of compliments followed by *for a . . .*
But I can choose not to see it at all,
as my white skin carries me like a sail.

If you flayed us, you'd notice only the sex,
but it's impossible to live without skin.
People are not books to be read
without a cover, people are impossible
to read, anyway.

Whenever I blurt the word "racist,"
I regret it, as when
I once called a child "illegitimate";
that night my husband asked,
"What difference does it make?"
Epithets are helicopters
with swords for blades,
but also methods of transport
from here to there.

At first, what our families didn't say or do
was not kind, and then we grew through it like a tree
whose roots invade sewer lines.
Good things—eating, learning, love—
depend on openings, penetration,
marriage.
So many ways to let the other in:
learn Spanish, eat grasshoppers, listen
to the rain on the roof and ask
if it falls harder for someone else.
So many ways to be placed outside:
woman, black, foreigner, Jew, gay, poor,
not us.

My words seep like water from ice.
You might wish for volcanoes,
a blaze of stars.
But in the cities where we live
almost no one stares.
Incidents are rare:
a drunk stumbling out of a bar spits,

a D.C. neighbor breathes "white bitch,"
every now and then.
Such things are mosquitoes,
waiting for a quick fist
to catch them, and wish.

Cross-Street

So much for the solid-
gold musical taste of the age,
                    upbeat, down
and out, love-
sick groans bawling
from the suitcase-sized boom box riding the shoulder
of a *cholo* in shades, webbed hairnet, flannel shirt
buttoned to the neck in midsummer, pimp-
strut rocking by on tip-
toe past pairs of squat, unisex
cops, hands on holsters, breezing as though the street's an open
bedroom, not book, closer
to sniffing whiffs of *Opium, Taboo,* off the dark necks' more darkly
bitten moons of unappeasable *chicas,* their wide, wing-
tipped eyes, salsa smiles night-shaded all
the way to the Bay of Angels...

On Mission Street's sizzling McMeat rack,
past a punk blond with spiked hair tufts
speaking Queen's English,—yakking
through a bull horn's snout in an apostolic fit for the sheer
thumping hell of it, zeal-crazed, hormone-hit,—a teenaged kid
brandishing a black Bible beats the air
over pedestrians' heads. Soon as gawking
girls stop to stare, his hoarse voice cracks; no less
than everyone dropping in their tracks, on their knees
at his feet, penitential sobs, mass conversion will do
in full view of the born-again street...

Through traffic and yak
without letup, listen: you can hear
those who promised to do away with history's
Alps on our backs now fighting for a place
in it; the old not letting go, the new
in tow, breaking
down, everywhere settling
for the nearest hole

to sink into,
                like anything pursued.

Gone & Gone

We meet   as always
on the corner of dusk & dark &
against that soubrettish tablet we step off
in search of the invisible night
that lurks inside of darkness
like a well-kept secret or a lie.

Wherever we are becomes a
carnival, a fair of the heart
with sidling glances at lust.
We knock down all the bottles
with one throw & are given a stuffed bear
so big we can hardly carry it.
We want to find someone to give it to:
there can be such hard waking in the world,
an ache inside every morning
& an ash to be raked at night.
But right now, if the streets cry out
at the awful crush & grind
we'll pick up more achievers,
new acquaintances of longing
& hold them to us
like limbs, like borrowed air
as we answer the wild siren call.

In the shadows where nothing is
reclaimed we romance on, each shot
getting easier to take on, put back,
shove off—crazed legs angling
toward the haphazard dawn.

We approach from every angle
& never arrive.
Across the street the light goes red.
Who are they trying to stop? Suddenly
we realize that like a person
who has seen more than ever happened
we are back where we began,
on the corner of dark & dawn,
elbows locked in place clutching
the prize of all those hours before.

Sometimes there are whole dreams
that come back, like the chorus
at the end of a song
or the sound of a cricket
trapped in the same field
each & every night—
its fevered rush toward morning,
the rest that comes with light.
We open our mouths to sing
& there is such crying to wake the world
that the humming of all-night diners
& laundromats will have to stop:
the great wailing surges up the avenue
like a brutish street-cleaning
or a spreading bruise toward the day.
We're parading in the discordant
lullaby, the cacophony of
this world & its creatures.

Our companions have fallen away, I turn
into the dawn's early dissonance
after dragging all night from one
face to another these unbearable
remains of a gift.
Everyone knows where they're going
until they're gone.

MARY CLARK

Parking

I got to know what was soft
and where the hard parts were

in that upholstered bedroom.
Every headlight was a worry.

I kept my clothes on as much
as I could. It didn't bother you.

Even that time getting caught didn't.
You liked it. You said you loved me,

but it was what I was doing
that you loved. You grabbed

at my hair when you said it.
I couldn't believe how fast

I didn't see you anymore.
Breath on the window blurs

the evergreens by the reservoir.
The fabric imprints my skin.

The engine, gasping, almost
stalling sometimes, rocks, still.

Pantyhose

When you wash them
do it gently
with a mild soap
and lightly
swish.
Silken, seamed,
off-black, mist, dotted,
patterned in some way,
support,
light support,
sheer, nude, coal,
reinforced toe,
taupe,
suntan, ivory,
smoke,
they're in there now
all crossed
over through
the small
accumulation
of bubbles
which gather
at the edges
of your porcelain
sink transformed
into something
womanly.
Rinse them fast
and hang
preferably
on an outdoor
clothesline
so that
if you stood

watching with a wide
imagination
and a generous
suspension
of disbelief,
you would see
something like
The Rockettes,
though certainly not
as shapely
and much more
out of unison.
When they dry
put them on
with well-filed
fingernails
in that way
women have
of rolling so quickly
a leg of nylon
into the ready position,
a rose into which
the foot steps
and all petals
unravel
evenly up the leg.

Making Up

Do it instinctively, like washing your hands or fumbling for your glasses on the night table in the morning, even though, for a small ritual, it is complicated, a minefield of subtleties, an act of aspiration, self-hatred, theatrics.

Stand before the full-length mirror on your closet door. You are dressed already, though your hair is still tangly and wet from the shower. You are wearing black tights and a long pink sweater your mother has picked out for you. It is one of the few things she has bought you that you actually like and are not ashamed to be seen in. You think it is funky, casual-but-cool, though a designer or your father (who likes you in long skirts and high collars) might tell you otherwise.

The refrain of a song goes through your head, threaded between your ears like a spool of film. It comes from your stereo in the living room. You know it so well, you don't even listen. *I can't get no sa-tis-fac-tion, I can't get no* . . . Flatter yourself. Think it is your theme song. Twenty-seven years ago, Mick Jagger wrote it just for you in anticipation of what you would be going through right here, right now.

The music vibrates through your auditory canals (still damp with shampoo) and against the aural nerves, which transmit it across the neurons and dendrites and synapses strung like telephone wires from your ears to your cerebral cortex, then send it down, down, down, into the depths of your gray brain matter, through the cerebellum, along your medulla oblongata to your central nervous system, branching out and down like tributaries from your night-cramped neck.

The music runs down the slope of your back, over those cute, fleshy mounds of your ass, down the lines of your thighs like seams on silk stockings, down the backs of your knees, along your calves to your pinkened heels and, finally, into your feet. Your feet! Your feet! Have them tap out the beat on the carpet, like door hinges, like flapping pancakes, like metronomes. Your senses, your whole body, are breathing: ears inhaling the sound, feet exhaling it on the floor. Become part of the rhythm, bopping, pacing yourself, surrendering to it. This will make you forfeit your own thoughts, which will suit you just fine.

No one, no one you know, makes up without music. Back in college, when you were half as poor, half as worldly and twice as confident, you and your friend Melissa had a whole intricate make-yourselves-up ceremony before every party. You would drink two bottles of white wine in her bedroom, listen to a dozen tapes on her boom box, try on fifteen outfits and take turns before the mirror. You would hand each other cosmetics as if they were surgical instruments: "Eyeliner." "Cover-up."

There were only certain songs you could listen to while you did your makeup—throbbing, juicy songs like "Beast of Burden" or "Diamond Dogs"—because these made you feel horny and flushed and seductive. Melissa was beautiful. Standing beside her in the mirror, you always looked puffy and dog-faced in comparison. But *you* could shimmy and dance: music did as much for you as cosmetics. Put it on and you could look okay. Most women know this, in fact. Go into our apartments. There's a tape player near the dresser, a radio propped up on the toilet tank.

As you move to the beat, confront your face. Do this critically, sucking in the cheekbones, pushing up the tip of your nose, eyeing your profile. Your nose is bulbous and a little lopsided. Your pores are big and rough-looking. You get funny laugh-lines around your mouth when you smile. Probe your chin for blackheads. Think that you look like your grandmother, the one with the collapsed face and gimp leg who came over from Poland. Know that this is not a nice thing to think. Since you are a feminist, vanity will always be a sticky issue with you. It is not, after all, politically correct.

You read an article once in a woman's magazine in which an aging writer argues yes, it's fine for a modern woman to get a face lift; there is nothing anti-feminist about cosmetic surgery. You disagreed with her vehemently: it smacked of rationalization, of shallowness and self-betrayal. "Aesthetic fascism," you called it.

And yet, you understand the longing for good skin, the pangs of ugliness, the desire to renovate a face. This is your dirty little secret. You want a nose job. You want liposuction. Children are dying of starvation in Somalia, on 145th Street, and you want liposuction.

But there is pain and there is paint, and the latter is much more user-friendly. The ancient Egyptians used kohl on their eyes. Tell yourself you are participating in a historical rite—almost archetypal behavior. (Slogan: "Look Jung forever?" You think not.) Put your undergraduate education to use. *All the world's a stage:* you are preparing to perform. *"There will be time to prepare a face to meet the faces you will meet..."* Besides—and you know this, really—makeup may be about beauty, conformity, consumerism, self-doubt and self-denial. But it's also a lot of fun. Example: Halloween.

Resign yourself to your features. Survey the terrain of your face blandly. The skin around your eyes and brows is always flaky and dry: psoriasis runs in your family. Squeeze the moisturizer onto your fingertips. It is pink and floral-smelling—a little too grandmothery for comfort. Massage it wildly over your face. The canvas is being gesso-ed, you think. You are an artist, a harlequin. Hell, you're a goddamn mime. The moisturizer was a free sample. It feels oily and false on your skin. Feathers could stick to it. You could be tarred and feathered with moisturizer. From inside your living room, the next song comes on the stereo. "Paint It Black." Think that this is not a bad idea.

The eyeliner is next, and this is the real arty part. Paint it on with a brush as thin as a needle, an exact, wispy stroke across the eyelid. It's easy on the right side, because you're right-handed, but for the left eyelid, your nose gets in the way and you have to contort your hand. It comes out too thick—you look slightly bruised. Wipe it off with your fingertip and start again. As an afterthought, make the lines extend out slightly from the corners of your eyes like Cleopatra. Hope you look more exotic than foolish. Then, take your eye pencil. With your fingertip, tug at the skin beneath your eye so that the bottom rim pulls away from the cornea. Think, "My, this looks attractive."

Draw a black line across the rim. You have done this since high school, so you can do it without even blinking, though when you do it to your friend Michael (in drag: fraternity prank), he will blink and flinch so violently you nearly jab him in the eye. "How do girls do that every day?" he will cry. For some reason, you will feel masterful.

You did not always wear eye pencil this way. When you were in high school, you wore it only halfway across your bottom lashes, in little retarded semicircles. You had read somewhere that this made your eyes look bigger. When you explained this to your friend Jeff, he said, "Really? Maybe I should draw a line halfway around my cock." You thought this was funny.

The last thing is lipstick. All this fussing, and you really do not wear much makeup. Some days there are eye shadow and mascara, but only if cocktail parties or authority figures are involved. Lipstick you love. Never mind how it looks, it feels sexy to apply. You can turn yourself on just putting on lipliner, teasing the rim of your mouth with a pencil. You never do actually get the line right: one bow of your upper lip is always higher and rounder than the other, the bottom goes crooked. But you fill it in with lipstick, slowly, feeling the waxy smoothness on your mouth, and it hovers there, announcing kisses, decorating your face, and for a minute you feel anointed and polished. This is something rarely talked about: the sensuousness of makeup, the way it makes you feel powerful.

Step back from the mirror. Your lips are a deep, brownish-red gash. You know you should blot them, but you have always loved color more than form. "Get Off of My Cloud" starts playing, and there you are, with your absurdly red lips, feeling costumed, feeling ready.

Milk Glass

My bathroom mirror is a window
with a sash I could throw open
if it were not painted shut.
Above it hangs a transparent pane
high enough to frame the sky.
Usually I forget this, as in the evening
while putting on my makeup
I am surprised by a streak of orange
or zigzag of dark wings headed for the sea.

Stepping from the shower, I see nothing
but vapor in the mirror
and in the square above, no telling
the difference between cloud
and condensation. I am nowhere
in this picture and everywhere at once
the way the blind woman sees:
pressing her face against milk glass.

This glass of misted silver breaks
my face apart, scatters all its light
the way the soul goes when it flies
out of the body, or music as it leaves
the tip of the conductor's baton
to begin its endless journey into space
where no one will ever say:
This was *The Swan of Tuonela*
by Sibelius who died at 92. This was
his cliff of cellos rising with vibrato
from the orchestra of death, beating
at his dark and rain-streaked window.

SHEP CLYMAN

Eternity Suffers From Distemper

The captain said over the loudspeaker,
"Ladies and gentlemen, welcome
to Los Angeles. There is no hope."
Each step a search for balance
with my friend, here for the first time,
beside me in his loose pants
and splayfooted saunter,
gliding over the sidewalk slabs
uprooted by trees or earthquakes
on which I've stumbled all my life.
He put his hand on my shoulder
once or twice. I felt as if
I were being lifted slightly.
My foot was hurting, he complained
of his back on Wilshire.
He said the two of us were like
the roots of a tree twisting through
the city. Los Angeles was my earth:
the loud clothes, the Sevillan
architecture inviting the sun,
the open sprawl of parks and people.
I had never loved my city before.
I was afraid of his left-handedness.
The sky was blue and sat heavy
on the squat buildings,
squeezing down between them like flesh,
holding the exhausted cars in place,
the drivers barely holding back.
Approximately my father's age, he frowned,
"There aren't any dogwoods in this city."
I was still laughing in the Fairfax district
and my friend, the only American Jew

to hate lox, was singing in Yiddish.
Someone's bubby asked him "Do you know
Auf den Pripechik?"
"No, my darling, how does it go?" he said
with the charm of one who believes
in the luck of his mistakes.
—It was night before we shuffled
through our fifth city to get downtown.
I was panting, my friend was singing,
we stopped at Cozy Court
where kids played in the dirt
between the bungalows, starlight
still finding them through
the roof of brown air and glass,
pressing into their cheeks its
reminding pricks from cold suns
hot without the distance; but it's the light,
it's the light that matters as it filters
all that way, through so much trouble
without a thought for itself, and maybe,
with a little luck,
one or two will not brush it off their cheeks
under the thick branches of
their parents' laughter killing
the waiting and the work,
killing the rotted bottoms
of bathtubs, killing a fifth.
We walked over a couple streets
and a huge green Holiday Inn sign
lit up against the night
Prime Rib Dinner $7.95
and the street was gray under the lamps,
as all great walls should be.

Faith

Maybe it happened as the first long earth-wave rolled through our town. Maybe it was later. We had aftershocks all night. Faith, my wife, wouldn't sleep inside. No one would but me. Everyone spent the night in the driveways on cots, or on the lawns in sleeping bags, as if this were a neighborhood slumber party. I think I had to prove to myself that if all else failed I could still believe in my own house. If that first shaker had not torn it to pieces, I reasoned, why should I be pushed around and bullied by these aftershocks rated so much lower on the Richter scale?

When the second big one hit us, just before dawn, I was alone and sleeping fitfully, pinned to my bed, dozing like a corporal in the combat zone waiting for the next burst of mortar fire. I sat up and listened to rafters groaning, calling out for mercy. I heard dishes leap and rattle in the kitchen. I listened to the seismic roar that comes rushing toward you like a mighty wind. I should have run for the doorjamb. I couldn't. I could not move, gripped by the cold truth of my own helplessness.

I sat there with the quilt thrown back and rode the tremor until the house settled down. Outside I heard voices. They rose in a long murmur of anxiety laced with relief, as children called to their parents, as neighbor talked to neighbor from lawn to lawn, from driveway to driveway. Eventually the voices subsided, and I was aware for the first time of a hollow place within, a small place I could almost put my finger on. Describing it now, I can say it felt as if a narrow hole had been scooped out, or drilled, right behind my sternum, toward the lower end of it, where the lower-most ribs come together.

At the time I had no words for this, nor did I try to find any. From the rising of the sun we had to take things one hour at a time. We were out of water. Sewage lines had burst, contaminating the mains. Phone lines were down. Power was out all over the county, and many roads were cut off. Long sections of roadbed had split. In the central shopping district, several older buildings, made of brick and never retrofitted, were in ruins. They'd been built on flood plain. As the tremor passed through it, the subsoil liquified. Faith and I live in a part of town built on solider stuff. No one's house jumped the foundation. But indoors, everything loose had landed on the floor—dishes, pictures, mirrors, lamps. Half our chimney fell into the yard. Every other house had a square hole in the roof or a chimney-shaped outline up one wall where the bricks once stood.

The next day I was working side by side with neighbors I had not talked with for weeks, in some cases, months. As we swapped stories and considered the losses, the costs, the federal help that might be coming in, I would often see in their eyes a startled and questioning fear that would send me inward to the place where whatever was now missing had once resided. I found myself wondering whether it was something new, or an old emptiness that had gone unnoticed for who knows how long. I'm still not sure.

By the third morning we had electricity again. We could boil water without building a campfire outside or cranking up the Coleman. I sat down at the kitchen table with a cup of coffee and I guess I just forgot to drink it. Faith sat down across from me and said, "What's the matter, Harry?"

"Nothing."

"Are you all right?"

"No, I'm not all right. Are you?"

"You've been sitting here for an hour."

"I don't know what to do. I can't figure out what to do next."

"Let's sell this place. Let's get out of here while we're still alive."

She looked like I felt. Along with everything else we were getting three or four aftershocks a day. It kept you on the ragged edge.

I said, "Where can we go?"

"Inland. Nevada. Arizona. I don't care."

"You said you could never live in Arizona."

"That was last year."

"The desert would drive you bananas, you said."

Halfway through that sentence, my voice broke. My eyes had filled with water. It would have been the easiest thing in the world to break into heaving sobs right there at the table.

"It's too hard," she said, "trying to clean up this mess and never know when another one's going to hit us. Who can live this way?"

"What does it feel like to have a nervous breakdown?" I said.

"Maybe all we need is a trip. I don't care where. Let's give ourselves a week, Harry, while we talk things over."

"That's not it."

"What's not it?"

I didn't answer. She waited and asked again, her voice on the rise, "What's not it? What's the matter, Harry? What's happening to us?"

Her eyes were blazing. Her mouth was stretched wide in a way I have learned to be wary of. It was not a smile. Faith has a kind of chiseled beauty. As the years go by, her nose, her cheeks, her black brows get sharper, especially when she's pushed. We were both ready to start shouting. Thirty more seconds we would be saying things we didn't mean. I didn't need a shouting match just then. Somehow she always prevails. Her background happens to be Irish and Mexican, a formidable combination when it's time to sling the words around.

Thankfully the phone rang. We hadn't heard it for so long, the jangle shocked us both. It was her mother, who had been trying to get through. Once they knew the houses were standing and no one had been injured, they talked on for half an hour or so, the mother mostly, repeating all the stories she'd been hearing, among them the story of a cousin with some acreage here in the county, where he grows lettuce and other row crops. Some men on the cousin's crew had recently come up from central Mexico on labor contracts, and one of them had asked for a morning off to take his wife to a local healer. During the quake the wife's soul had left her body, or so she feared, and this healer had ways to bring a soul back. Faith's mother reminded her that after the big one in Mexico City back in 1987, numerous stories had drifted north, stories of people who found themselves alive and walking around among the ruins, while inside something had disappeared.

I still have to wonder why the mother called when she did. Whether it was by chance or by design, I still can't say. Probably a little of both. She claims to have rare intuitive powers. This healer, the *curandera,* happened to be a woman she knew by name and had been visiting for a year or so, ever since her husband had passed away. Faith had been visiting her, too. Her skills, they said, remedied much more than ailments of the flesh.

As soon as her mother hung up, Faith repeated the story of the field worker's wife. It came with an odd sort of pressure, as if she were testing my ability to grasp its importance. I don't know. I'm still piecing that day together. Maybe Faith, too, was feeling some form of inexpressible loss, and maybe she, too, was groping for a way to voice it.

"This healer," I said, "what does she do?"

"It's hard to explain."

"Is it some kind of Catholic thing? The devil creeping in to steal your soul away?"

She shook her head. "I don't think it's like good spirits and evil spirits or anything along those lines."

"What is it, then?"

"Maybe it's like the door of your life springs open for a second."

"Why do you say that?"

"Maybe your soul flies out and the door slams shut again."

"You think that can happen?"

"I'm just thinking out loud."

"It's a hell of a thing to say."

"Don't look at me that way."

"Just tell me if you believe something like that could happen."

"You hear people talk about it."

"When are you going down there again?"

"Sometime soon, I hope. It would be a good time for a treatment."

"Is that what they call it?"

"You can call it whatever you want."

"A treatment? That sounds like..."

"Like what?"

"Some kind of medical deal."

"Please, Harry. If you're going to get defensive, I don't want to talk about it."

"I'm not defensive."

"Your guard goes up."

"Gimme a goddamn break, Faith!"

"I can feel it, Harry! You know I can!"

My guard goes up. What guard, I was thinking. I had no guards left. That was the problem. Everything I had ever used to defend myself or support myself was gone. I was skidding. That's how I felt. Supportless. I had to get out of there. I had to think. Or perhaps I had to get out of there and not-think.

I took off for the hardware store, to pick up some new brackets for the bookshelves. I switched on one of the talk shows out of San Francisco. The guest was a trauma counselor. The theme was, "Living With the Fault Line." Someone had just called in a question about betrayal.

"Can you give me an example?" the counselor said.

"Maybe that isn't the right word," the caller said.

"You feel like something has been taken away from you." It wasn't a question.

"It's almost like my body opened up and something escaped."

A long chill prickled my arms, my neck. I had just reached the hardware store. I pulled into the parking lot, switched off the engine, and turned up the sound.

"That's big," the talk show host said. "That's major."

"Hey," said the counselor, "let's think about it together for a minute."

"Think about what?" the host said. "Betrayal?"

"The earth. Think about the umbilical tie. From your mother, to your grandmother, and on down the line. On back through the generations to whatever life forms preceded ours. Sooner or later we all have to trace our ancestry to this nurturing earth, and meanwhile we have laid out these roads and trails and highways and conduit pipes and bridges and so forth in full faith that she is stable and can be relied upon. You follow me? Then when she all of a sudden gives way, splits open, lets off this destructive power without even the little advance notice you get for a hurricane or a killer blizzard, why, it's like your ground wire disconnects. It's so random...you realize how we're all just hanging out here in empty space. Believe me, folks, you're not alone. I've been feeling this way myself for days..."

He had a low, compelling voice that sent buzzes through me. I was tingling almost to the point of nausea. The tears I had not been able to release in the kitchen now began to flow. I sat in the hardware store parking lot weeping the way a young child lost on a city street might weep for the missing parents.

When my tears subsided, I tried to call the house. The line was busy. I started driving south, sticking to roads I knew were open, more or less following a route I'd followed once before, on a day when Faith's car was in the shop and she needed a ride. It only takes twenty minutes, but you enter another world. Down at that end of the county it's still mostly fertile delta land. From the highway you look for a Burger King and a Stop-N-Go. Past a tract of duplexes you enter an older neighborhood of bungalows and windblown frame houses from the 1920s and earlier. The street leading to her cottage was semi-paved. Beyond the yard, row crops went for a mile across broad, flat bottomland—lettuce, chard, broccoli, onions. The grass in the yard was pale and dry. Low cactus had been planted next to the porch.

The fellow who answered my knock said he was her son, Arnoldo, lean and swarthy and watchful. He wore jeans and dusty boots, as if he might have just walked in by another door. When I mentioned my wife's name he did not seem impressed. Anglos never came to see this woman. In his eyes I could have been an infiltrator from County Health, or from Immigration, or someone shaking them down for a license. When I mentioned my mother-in-law's family name, he softened a little. Dredging up some high school Spanish, I tried to describe my symptoms. Arnoldo spoke a little English, but not much. I touched my chest.

"Mi alma," I said. "Después del temblor, tengo mucho miedo. Es posible que mi alma..."

"Ha volado?" he said. Has flown away?

"Sí. Comprende?"

He looked at me for quite a while, making up his mind. He looked beyond me toward the curb, checking out the car. At last he stepped aside and admitted me into a small living room where a young mother and her son were sitting on a well-worn sofa. There was a TV set, a low table with some Spanish-language magazines, a sideboard with three or four generations of family photos framed. In one corner, votive candles flickered in front of an image of the blue-robed, brown-faced Virgin of Guadalupe. Between this room and a kitchen there was a short hallway where a door now opened. A moment later a pregnant woman appeared, followed by an older woman, short and round and very dark. She stopped and looked at me while Arnoldo explained the family tie. The names seemed to light her face with a tiny smile of recognition. I heard him mutter, *"Susto."* A scare. She nodded and said to me, *"Bienvenidos."* Welcome. Please make yourself at home.

She beckoned to the woman on the sofa and the son, who limped as he started down the hallway. The rear door closed, and Arnoldo offered me a chair. I couldn't sit. I was shivering. I made him nervous. I was sure he regretted letting me inside. He pointed to a long, jagged lightning streak of a crack across the sheetrock wall behind the TV set. *"El temblor,"* he said. The earthquake.

Again, I pointed at my chest. *"El temblor."*

We both laughed quiet, courteous laughs and looked away. I sat down then, though I could not bear the thought of waiting. This was crazy. I was out of control. What was I doing? What did I think would happen? I remembered the day I'd driven over there with Faith and parked at the curb. I remembered the glow on her face and how I had extinguished the glow. She had wanted me to come inside with her. "What for?" I said. "There's nothing wrong with me." The idea filled me with resentment. "It's not a lot of money, Harry," she had said. "She doesn't charge. You just leave something on the table, whatever you feel like leaving."

It wasn't the money. It was the strangeness of being there with her. Faith has these dramatic, mixed-blood looks that have kept people guessing, and have kept me guessing, too, I suppose. Greek? they ask. Portuguese? Italian? Black Irish? Mexico has always been somewhere on that list, but when we first started dating she would never have emphasized it. Her Spanish was no better than mine. Faith McCarthy was her maiden name. Suddenly I did not know this woman. Mexican on her mother's side, that was one thing. Going into the barrio to visit healers, that was something else. I wasn't ready for that. When did it start? Where would it lead? I remembered the rush of dread that day in the car as I realized I was looking at a complete stranger who was inviting me to some place I had never been.

Sitting there with Arnoldo I felt it again, the dread of strangeness. Who was he, after all, with his boots and his lidded eyes? Her son? He could be anyone. What if this was the wrong house? I heard voices from the hallway. Then the young mother and the limping boy passed through the living room, out the front door, and the healer was beckoning to me. I, too, was limping, crippled with doubt. I had no will. I followed her to another room, with a backyard view across the fields, once a bedroom, now furnished with a chest of drawers, a couple of chairs, a long couch with a raised headrest. She didn't speak for quite some time. She just looked at me. She was no more than five feet tall, her hair silver, pulled back in a short braid. I guessed she was in her sixties, her body thick and sturdy, covered by a plain dress with short sleeves that left her arms free. Her face was neutral, neither smiling nor frowning. Her eyes seemed to enter me, black eyes, the kind that go back in time, channels of memory. She knew my fear. She knew everything about me.

She asked me to take off my shoes and my shirt, nodding toward a chair before she turned away, as if occupied with some small preparation on top of the chest. My panic welled up. It was mad to be doing this, stripping down at the edge of a broccoli field, inside the house of people I'd never seen before. I imagined the old woman asking me to swallow something terrible. Above the chest a shelf was lined with jars and small pouches. Who knew what they contained? My panic turned to fury. I could have taken the old woman by the throat. I wanted to. She knew too much. Maybe I began to understand hysteria just then, how a person can start to spin around and fly to pieces. Why didn't I spin? Why didn't I run? I stood there swearing that if she tried to give me something, I would not swallow it. That was the little contract I made with myself as I lay down on the long couch.

She covered me to my neck with a sheet. From a pouch tied around her waist she withdrew a clump of leafy fragrant stems and waved it up and down the length of my body. Her lips moved but made no sound. She leaned in close, pushing her thumbs across my forehead, digging into the furrows there, digging in close to my eyes. She began to speak, a soft murmur of words that were not Spanish. Later on, Faith's mother would tell me these may have been Yaqui words, a Yaqui incantation. There is something to be said for not knowing the literal meaning of words. If you trust the speaker to be using them in the proper way, it makes it easier to surrender. You can surrender to the sound. Is that what was happening? Did I trust the sound of the *curandera*'s voice? Let's say I wanted to. Let's say my need to trust her outweighed my fear. Who else could I have turned to? In her hands I began to drift. I would not say she put me to sleep. I was not asleep. I did not feel asleep. I just wasn't entirely awake. My eyes weren't open. But I was still aware of being in the room. I was outside the room, yet in it, too, listening to her gentle voice.

While her hands worked on my forehead, my temples, my eyes, my nose and cheeks, her voice became the voice of wings, large and black and wide as the couch, as wide as the room, as wide as the house, sheets of darkness moving toward me, undulating, until I saw that these were the wings of an enormous bird, a dark eagle or a condor hovering. It finally settled on my chest, its feet on my skin so I could feel the talons. They held me as if in the grip of two great hands. They dug in. They were on my chest and inside my chest. From the talon grip I understood some things about this bird. I knew its solitary drifting on the high thermal currents, soaring, waiting. I knew its hunger. I knew the power of the beak. When the flapping of the wings increased, I wasn't surprised. They made a flapping thunder that sent a quiver through me, then a long shudder, then a shaking as sudden and as terrifying as the shaking of the earth, with a sound somewhere inside it, the slap of a ship's sails exploding in a gale. I was held by the chest and shaken by this huge bird until my body went slack, exhausted by the effort to resist. In that same moment the wings relaxed. The hold upon my chest relaxed. I watched the bird lift without any motion of the wings, as if riding an updraft. It hovered a while, and I had never felt so calm. A way had been cleared at last, that's how it felt. Everything had been rattled loose again and somehow shaken into place. A rim of light edged the silhouette of dusky feathers. I saw the fierce beak open as if about to speak. Its piercing cry almost stopped my heart.

My eyes sprang wide. The woman's dark brown face was very close. The heel of her hand had just landed on my forehead with a whack. Her black eyes were fixed on mine. What did I see there? Who did I see?

When I got back home Faith met me at the door. She, too, had been crying. I'd been gone maybe three hours. She stood close and put her arms around me. We didn't speak. We looked at each other. In her face I recognized something I would not, until that afternoon, have been able to identify. Her eyes were like the old woman's eyes, that same fierce and penetrating tenderness. It swept me away. We kissed as if we had not seen each other in weeks, as if we had had the fight that nearly happened and we were finally making up. It was a great kiss, the best in years. It sent us lunging for the bedroom where we made love for the first time in many days.

In our haste we forgot to pull the curtains. Afternoon light was pouring through the windows. At first she was bathed in light, though as we thrashed and rolled she seemed to be moving in and out of shadow. Then she was above me and so close she blocked the light. As she rose and fell and rose and fell I could only see her outline. When she abruptly reared back, her arms were wings spread wide against the brightness, while she called out words I could scarcely hear. A roaring had filled my ears. A thousand creatures were swarming towards the house, or a storm-driven wind. Maybe it was another aftershock. Maybe it was the pounding of my own blood.

"Oh! Oh! Harry!" Her voice came through the roar. "Harry! Harry!" as if I were heading out the door again. Had I been able to speak I would have called to her. Maybe I did call. I know I heard my voice. "I'm here!" I cried. "I'm here! I'm here!"

JANE HIRSHFIELD

The Window

I am not—
opened or closed—
what you expected, o heart.

Or would you
without me have thought
to throw open
the flooding and roar,
to step through the lion's gold pelt?

have thought that
the passionate glass is the body?
and this life, the one life you wanted?

Wanted,
meaning neither *lacked,*
nor *desired,*
but something else...
something closer
to how, when the two owl-lovers
begin their night singing
and all the black length of the woods
is held in those arms,
not one stone, not one leaf goes uncalling.

If I had been what you thought,
o heart,
how could the clear glass
flow as it does with mountains,

with jewel-colored, perishing fish?
flashing and falling,
the black-bright rain of beings and things?

Some recognizable, yours, but others—
too fleeting or large—that cannot be spoken.

Though the one world touches the other
in every part, o heart,
in silence,
like new lovers taking their fill in the crowded dark.

The Tea Light of Late September

As if the porous bag
had been dipped
once, twice,
once more
in the summer's water,
then set aside.
Halfway between
sleep and waking,
I took it between my lips.
And though the earth
is everywhere terrible
and cruel,
the heart diamond flashed out
once, twice, and once again
the semaphore-reply
it cannot help but make to beauty,
before the bone-white cup
is fully drained.

The Fish

There is a fish
that stitches
the inner water
and the outer water together.

Bastes them
with its gold body's flowing.

A heavy thread
follows that transparent river,
secures it—
the broad world we make daily,
daily give ourselves to.

Neither imagined
nor unimagined,
neither winged nor finned,
we walk the luminous seam.
Knot it.
Flow back into the open gills.

DAVID MAMET

The Waterworld

But did we not
Mint our excuse to sin,
And nurture it to our advantage?

Now here, now there,
Like drops on a pond
Shot by the needlegun
From the silt to the surface; now
The mechanism of our thought
Leaps in reverse
Like that hid engine of the waterworld.

Philosophers all, then we pray:
Goad us to acceptance
Until our scoured resignation,
Bleached in loathing,
License our longing for revenge.

The World From Under

The dream rises and falls like the breath
of a sleeper in long smooth mirroring
waves. My mother

arises, presses against
the surface of the water, which to her
appears a flat gold-leafed roof or
sky. But for my part I can see her figure

made responsible by the water,
no longer mirror-black and reckless,
but a deep placental purple-
blue. You, too, could see her leaning into

the world from under. You see how
her head is about to break the surface
that forms a wall around her?
You see how the water wraps

her head like a new skin or glove?
She is a thing protruding. She
is a fully formed enigma. You see
how that's my mother under there?

Nicholas by the River

Two heaps of clothes by an old stump,
and Nicholas neck-deep in that water
too cold for our own good. Shimmering
when he said he wasn't sure but thought
maybe it was a man he wanted,
though I was what he had
under his hands in that blue current.
Blue of the nearly and almost.
Darker blues in the middle
over the deep spots. Nearly the end
of eighteen, and too late in August not
to expect even that which I'd been denied.

Upriver a couple hundred yards
an old man dropped his hook & sinker
and was already watching it drift away
when he saw us—our pair of heads
like two white rocks at the river's edge.
So nothing need have gone much
further. No one need have groped
in the furious currents, or the lovely
lazy fish have come to harm in our close
proximity. And I might not have taken my friend
around behind the craggy jut of rocks
and bent over him as he lay back
shivering in the sun. Maybe
it was not even necessary for him
to moan a little and turn me
from him, bend me forward, head
down, hair dragging the water,
so he could enter me the only way
he knew, saying sorry sorry sorry.

Insemination Tango

A man in the south of France flaps his elbows
and dances with a female crane, who is
the last of the Black-tails. He hoots
and coos, and she lowers her long
delicate neck. Yesterday the man had sunned
and swum amid a swarm of nude swimmers
in the Riviera's cloudy waters, so that now
his skin shines pink, his bald spot
darkened. He lifts his arms, and the bird
lifts her wings. He struts, high-stepping
across the pen in which she's lived her whole
life, and has come to allow this display
of a man's possible desire. The flutter
of black tail feathers raised: her iridescent
acquiescence. That low sweeping squawk:
her answer of longing. And though the man's
response is silly, strange, and sadly
wrong, it will do to stir her enough—
so that whatever he's hiding, whatever he's holding
in his clenched flailing fist like a secret
kept too long alone, she can finally let him
let go—now that she's ready to stand still
and take whatever that love is he's giving.

Paris Subway Tango

Somebody almost walked off
with all my stuff
—Ntozake Shange

at best you can say
your judgment was tainted
by movies and old
expectations
    Paris equals passion
    n'est pas?   so why not ride
              the subway just this one
              night despite
              all the echoes of caution
              dancin : in your head
              and how even in Harlem
              you have a thousand
reasons to stay above
ground instead
of ruttin : beneath
the fabric of some city
that seems clipped
from a Romare Bearden
nightmare book
    but this is Paris
    Chagall and Degas
and men whose eyes fill
with mysteries
of North African deserts
              so the first brush
              of body against body
and you get this wild rush
of good sense fightin : desire
yellin : *I want**I don't want*
like salt messin : with perfume

and although his face
flirts with your imagination
his hand's dippin : into your purse
so, baby, you fling aside all caution
lay him out with a one-two step
swingin : hip to hip
like when you used to
Arthur-Murray-in-a-hurry
    part Hustle : part Hucklebuck
    matchin : his every tightass turn
    groovin : between track and train
        like the two of you been
        practicin : M*T*V
except your purse is the cash prize
so do it, girl, cause
maybe this home-boy-arab
don't know you
ain't takin : no shit
even if you gotta tango
on this metro clear to the end

Caution: This Woman Brakes for Memories

When the air is thin with frost
I blow rings of ice smoke
as I did when I was young
and imagined myself grown
and never answering to anyone.
From smoke rings to pots
that became helmets and tanks,
I play-acted a world where
color held no name and eyes
were tears holding light.

Without knowing the contours
of earth, any rock
can become mountain, and puddles
vast oceans of many-legged beasts.
None of this is new.
All children are urged
to wander through the screen
of what is real before
they are pushed into the serious
matter of living where they lose
the surprise of believing.

We become adults with only a toehold
on fantasy, like ghost light from a torn retina
vanishing in the corner of the eye where, half
blind, we learn when to turn a phrase or bend
a letter until *o* becomes *e* or *3*
evolves into *8* and less simple digits.
No easy idiot graffiti of *girl*
into *gril,* but *loan*
into *god* and *home* into *bog.*
One blink and a sign that reads
Warning: Truck Makes Wide Turns

can be misread as *Caution: This
Woman Breaks for Every Turn*
and everything is possible.

Yesterday as I crossed the flag-
stones of a posh hotel foyer
I saw a fat rat gray and sleek
claws clicking like loose chains
on the slick tiles when he moved.
I heard him yell: *Look at me go in and out
of revolving doors, go pitty pat
on my rat-like feet, go into fake
sunshine and champagne and home.*
The silk calla lilies nodded yes
and I believed them.

Today on the beach at La Push, logs became
chairs, dead bears, boats with roots like stars and
I was a ship sailing back to the beginning.

Mad Girls, Ghosts, Grace, and the Big Break in the City of Sisterly Love

I'll tell you what I know. Although my name is in that wonderful program—"Melissa Halliday" is me, right there under "Principals"—I know myself enough to know that my shining moment was a mistake, which is okay since my mother taught me self-respect, my father taught me common sense, and living with my brother has put the fear of God into me about being stupid. I'm only sixteen, but I know all about this cut-throat business I'm in; it's *hard*, especially for a girl, and especially for a black girl with not enough ambition. I learned that from Caitlin, right before she got her wish to get out of Philadelphia and disappeared back to New York. I know I'm only a good dancer, not great, not even really good. I know I wouldn't have gotten the chance without her, without that messed-up thing she did to get me my moment in the sun.

And although I haven't got everything figured out yet, here's what else I know about it.

It's a boiling July Saturday afternoon when me and Caitlin are sitting out on the nasty old brown carpet in the hallway downstairs at Philidance, right underneath that poster with the quote—I don't know who said it—"Those who dance are thought mad by those who hear not the music." I've always thought it was corny, but a lot of girls like it. Anyway, we're sweating half to death since the company's too damn cheap to turn on the air conditioning except a little bit in the dance studios. As usual, the other girls have gone to the diner across the street where the air is on, but me and Caitlin are in the hot seat, ordered to stay close-by; besides, Philidance is pretty cliquey and Caitlin doesn't get along with people so well.

"Only in this ass-backward, white-bread *Philadelphia*," Caitlin growls, *so* pissed off, in her put-on old lady voice like a cross between Moms Mabley and Flip Wilson. "We all get shoved out of rehearsal because Little Miss Diva can't hack it and starts bawling like a baby on Meredith's shoulder. At Ailey—"

"I know, Caitlin," I say. "I know all about you and Alvin Ailey."

Caitlin's all hunched over yanking off a toenail with her teeth, and she's grumbling things like "Ain't nothing but politics when a whiny, no-talent, arhythmic, billboard-assed, limp little bitch of a bunhead blimp like that takes *my* solo," and although I don't agree I whistle, marveling how ferociously she can jam on insults when she doesn't like someone. I don't get involved, except I can sort of see her point, so I say, "Hmm."

She pops her toe out of her lips and spits a flake across the hallway. "That all you can ever say is 'Hmm'?"

"No," I say, not about to get into it. "Gimme a Newport," I say. She just rolls her big green eyes, takes her foot flat in both hands like a piece a Wonder Bread, shoves it back in again, and mumbles with a mouthful of foot, "Gedit y'own dan self!" So I go into her dance bag and shove aside her sweaty garbage, and I see inside she's got a nine-pack of rubbers, which I hold up to her.

Still chewing, she says, "Least I got a use for them." I think, Yeah, at least she's got a use for them, but I only say, "With all them bobby pins and junk in your bag, they've got holes in them anyway." She looks at me funny for a second, then breaks up chuckling when I put the butt between my lips and try to flick my empty Bic.

"Damn, girl, gimme that! Don't you know how to suck? 'Course not, you nasty old clam-licking sex pervert. I'll show you." She rips the butt away, pops it in her lush lips, and bugs her eyes out crazily, making sex sounds. I laugh and laugh, and we fall all over each other acting giddy and I just love her. Even the way she always talks like a construction worker—I mean, "bitch" and "nigger" and "faggot" and "douche bag" are her greatest terms of endearment—but I just chalk that up to her being from New York. She's older than me, almost seventeen, and I just imagine she must have seen some things. Besides, I like her rough edges. They keep her from being too perfect.

Don't think that I worshipped her, though; we disagreed on lots of things. For one, I'm a ballerina of sorts, and Caitlin thought ballet the wimpiest form of dance ever invented. For another, she had a nearly insane paranoia about lesbians, so strong it made you wonder. Well, okay, there *are* lots of gay women in this company, and I suppose that's what really got her in trouble from day one, mouthing off about it in front of Meredith, the ballet teacher—"clam lickers" this and "muff divers" that. This certainly didn't win Caitlin many friends here. She never explained it, but my theory is it's something to do with her mother. They don't have the best relationship, and Caitlin sometimes mentioned her mom's "friends," and I never heard her say one word about her dad. I always would tell her she picked the wrong profession then, but she wouldn't hear it. When she kidded me about being one, I would say, "Unlike you, Caitlin, I am not a natural dancer, my parents are not rich, I go to school still, and I work at waitressing to pay for classes and have no time or energy for *any* social life at all. So how do you suppose I manage to be gay? Also, I'm not gay because I'm a virgin, and frankly in no hurry." She would tease me but that's all, saying, "Philadelphian, virgin—same thing."

So, while rolling around on each other laughing, we hear Miss Diva let out a wail inside the studio, and Caitlin becomes all serious again and picks herself off of me. "Damn," she says, pulling down her wiry, burnt sienna–colored hair, "we're gonna be waiting here for *hours.*" She holds the lit cigarette out to me. I don't say, "It's your own fault," but instead I try to cheer her up.

"I'm not smoking that," I say, "with your spit and toe-jam all over it."

She just huffs, pulls up her knees to her chest, and knocks her head back against the wall. We listen to her competitor crying inside for a while. Caitlin looks to the ceiling, French-inhales, and blows a smoke ring, then another little one through that. Her eyes are almost Asian-shaped, olive-green grooved with brown flecks like the underside of a mushroom. She looks dignified and sad, but I don't think she's sorry.

"Please stop gawking at me, Trina," she says. While my name is Melissa, that's Mel, "Trina" is short for "Ballet-Katrina," which is another name like "bunhead" that the modern dancers call people like me and Miss Diva.

"I can't help it," I admit. I tell her yet again I think she's the most beautiful dancer in class. When she says which class, I say, "Modern, jazz, *and* ethnic."

It's not that she can't be a beautiful ballerina, too, if she wanted, it's just that she doesn't want to; she's got fantastic technique, God-given lines, perfect extension, and strong arches, but she thinks ballet's boring. She lifts weights and is lean without being all emaciated and anorectic; unlike me, she has a woman's body already—her breasts are not bumps, and there's no mistaking her from behind for a little boy. But she has no weight problem and can eat whatever she wants, and I sometimes hate her for that. And it's true that Caitlin should easily be a soloist at least in the second company; and I suppose it's also true that Miss Diva is slightly baby-fatty and ugly and only got the role because she's tall and the token white girl in our section and cries like nobody's business.

And so I'm watching gorgeous Caitlin blow smoke rings, and working myself up to being outraged on her behalf, when the door to the studio opens and Meredith steps out into the hall followed by a sniffling Miss Diva, who's rubbing her knee where she fell on it when Caitlin tripped her. Meredith is a Trina-type, and her one eyebrow is slanted into a furious V as she glares down at me and says, "You should know better, Mel," and then turns to Caitlin. "You," she says, pointing, steaming, then giving up, "just you better be in my office in five minutes, girl." Caitlin blows out a billow of smoke and shrugs; I think this is no time for her to be defiant. Then, I know it's also true that Caitlin is just a plain big mouth with too much attitude, which is what landed us out here in the hall in the first place and ensured that she would never get her solo at this company.

I look over at Julianna—to give Miss Diva her real name—and see her face flushed like pink lemonade, her eyelids swollen, her forehead all pimply from using too much hairspray to mat her hair back, her clavicle bones protruding, her thin chapped lips quivering. I'm thinking, She's what they want, the kind of ballerina people like the old folks at the Academy of Music will pay money to see. I'm thinking, Our local ballet company has never had a black woman Cinderella or Swan. But I'm also thinking what a bloodthirsty business I'm in, and almost feel lucky that I'll probably never get beyond the corps or maybe a Sugar Plum Fairy. Almost lucky.

I eye Julianna and think she could use a little paint on her face. "Ug-leeeee!" is how Caitlin put it once, going off on the new girl with an old Moms routine. "Her face is sooo ugly, chile, honest to goodness it hurts my feelings!" An exaggeration, I think, but then Julianna does look so sickly: always talks soft like she can't breathe, holds her head or stomach like she's carrying around a whopping migraine or constant cramps. She's thin enough to wear that pink leotard and those shrinkwrapped Levi's, but her skin is soft and puffy like a child's, making her look fatter than she is. As I've seen her do so many times before, Julianna nervously puts one hand over her ear, as if simple footsteps sounded to her like thunder; I see that the knobby tip of her elbow is blotched with freckles. I try to be generous, but next to Caitlin she looks like a big, gawky white mouse.

Philidance is no place for the kinds of ballerinas people pay money to see.

Meredith turns from us and starts down the hall. Julianna waits for a second, then follows, shaking, unable to look at us. As she's passing, Caitlin sticks out a foot to trip her, just as she did in rehearsal, and starts singing "Ebony and Ivory." Julianna manages to hop over, but Meredith swings around, yanks Caitlin up by the collar of her sweatshirt, and knocks the Newport out of her mouth onto the brown rug, where it starts to make a stink like burning plastic.

"That's supposed to be funny?" Meredith says, her thin face looking haunted like a mummy's.

"*I* think so," says Caitlin, not blinking.

I'm afraid Meredith will pound her, but she just stands there shaking, clutching Caitlin's shirt for a long time. Behind them, Julianna starts sniffling again. Then Meredith says, "We'll see about that, Caitlin," and releases her grip. She puts her arm around Julianna, and says, "I don't know what's wrong with you girls, you're like animals," and heads down the hall again. I'm uneasy that she includes me in the statement, and feel lousy all the way around.

"They must be fucking," Caitlin whispers to me, still posing, staring after them, but I can tell she's nervous. She slumps to the floor beside me and watches them walking away, both looking so awkward, tiny Meredith in her black unitard holding beanpole Julianna in her too-tight jeans.

"Look at her twist-twat," Caitlin hisses to me, meaning the way the crotch seam of Julianna's pants are so tight, it seems you can see her privates. But this is not funny to me now—I've got no place to go but Philidance—and I stand up.

"Where're you going?" she asks, grabbing my elbow.

"I'm going in to practice," I say. "Some of us do that, you know."

"I'll go with you," she says, hauling up her big bag covered with buttons from Broadway shows and stickers with dancewear logos, stuffed so full of rubbers and sweaty things it's half as big as she is. I think to say, "Uh uh, you've got to go get yours from Meredith," but I can't talk.

We walk into the studio smelling of rosin dust and coffee and sweat, and turn on the overhead lights. Caitlin pushes into the sprung floorboards with her feet; the movement is as natural for her as blinking. We walk through the choreography, quiet, me watching her in the mirror, and her watching her in the mirror. And she says, "I'm a better dancer than her, right?" I answer yes. "I'm better looking, I know that," she laughs. We mark the phrase one more time, and she says, "And I belong here more than her." I watch her carefully, trying to figure her. She begins to whip around, not marking but really dancing, like a . . . like a what? A juggernaut. She sweeps across the room to the mirror, stops, and lifts her right leg until her flexed foot touches her ear. Without looking at me, she says, "And so do you."

"That's right," I say. "And I've got nowhere else to go. So I don't need you making waves for me. You know?"

"Did you ever think about moving to New York?" she says. "Wouldn't that be fun, you and me, living together in New York? Like sisters. My mother would get us an apartment in the Village—hmm, she'd just *love* you." She places her leg down and looks at me. I see she doesn't think much of what she sees. "You could get into Ailey with me," she tries. I frown. "I'd help you," she says. "What do you think?"

"I think that's stupid," I say. At that moment, we hear Meredith's voice calling down the hall. Mad. Caitlin smacks the mirror with her flat palm, spins out a fierce pirouette, then walks up to me, breathing angrily.

I shake my head, and say, "Your dancing's fine, Caitlin; it's your big mouth that's the problem. Don't say anything stupid to her in there, okay? At least for me, think about *me*."

"I do think about you. We're best friends, aren't we? I take care of you, don't I?"

I pause, I think about it. For some reason, it's hard for me to commit myself. We hear Meredith yell again, angrier. Caitlin goes on alert, looks to the door, slaps me with a glance from those olive eyes, and I can tell my answer is important to her. My throat squeezes shut, but I finally get it out—"Yeah." She seems to grow five inches; she grabs the strap of her bag like she's strangling it. I say, "Just be calm, don't get her madder, okay? Don't mess up this show for me, okay?"

But like a machine, Caitlin switches on attitude. Posing with one hand on a hip like a runway model, the other hand flying in an arc of rapid-fire snapping fingers, she says, "I'm willing to be a little fish in a big pond, or a big fish in a little pond. I am *not* going to be treated like a little fish in a little pond. Step aside, douche bag. Madame goes to work."

She brushes by me, pinches my rear hard, and says, "I'm going to dance this solo."

"Not if you get kicked out," I say.

"Then you'll get your big break."

Being a little fish in a little pond myself, I didn't know what she meant. I didn't think. I didn't know what it was like to be a threat to anybody, and I didn't know what it was like to be a shark out there with other sharks. I looked Caitlin square in those big, luscious eyes and knew she was up to no good, but all I could say was, "Hmm."

Although I was dying to listen in, I stayed in the studio to dance off my shot nerves by marking the choreography again by myself. I was hungry for this performance; that's what makes me feel guilty about the whole thing. Caitlin didn't need it—she would go on to wow everybody in a hundred beautiful dances. But me, I guessed I only had this one, or at most maybe two more until my senior year, when I'd start getting ready for college. Not to say that I didn't have fantasies. I'm a realist, though. My favorite thing, really, is just to dance by myself. I don't even need to look in the mirror. I may not look beautiful, but I can feel beautiful.

The night I fell in love with ballet was the same night I realized I would never be a dancer. My parents made me take classes since I was nine. I had little recitals and stuff and I was okay, but in ballet, okay is already not good enough even for a nine-year-old. But then they took me for my twelfth birthday to the outdoor theater at the Mann Music Center to see Gelsey Kirkland in *The Sleepwalker*. I remember feeling each delicate step like a kick in my stomach, and crying all the way to the end so my parents had to carry me out to the parking lot. I drove them crazy all the way home, still crying until I went to bed that night. I made them buy me a video of it for Christmas, and I often fast-forward to the part where Gelsey, walking in her sleep, floats down the stairs, *en pointe*, carrying a man's body in her arms, in her nightgown looking like a ghost. I force myself to watch it over and over again sometimes; even though it kills me, I can't help it, like you can't help picking off a scab. I knew that first time watching her I would never, ever, ever be that graceful.

I know this for a fact, and I know all about hunger. People go to see ballet like they want to have a good dream, hungry for the "mystique" and all that, angry if they don't get it. But now, after some years at it, I watch Gelsey and know that although she looks graceful, it doesn't *feel* graceful at all with your toes crushed up feeling like they're being sucked down a bathtub drain; being a stick but only seeing in the mirror a fat bull toad; you got girls that barely have their periods taking drugs and talking like used old maids, weary, trying to be strong as a man and act like a woman and look like a child and dance like a ghost in a dream. Now, Caitlin doesn't understand about that, but she could *do* it.

So that's what I'm thinking then, feeling angry at Caitlin for wasting time—mine and hers—when I hear the shouting echoing down the corridor. A door slams, and I step into the hall—no sign of Meredith or Julianna or any of the other girls yet, only Caitlin standing by the locker-room door, her head down.

"Rehearsal's canceled," she says, her voice scratchy like she has laryngitis. She goes inside, and even though I don't really want to be, I am pulled after her.

The locker room is dark and dead quiet and cluttered with junk like a robber's cave. Usually, it's full of the girls chattering away, sounding like the exotic birdhouse at the Fairmount Zoo. It just about smells like that, too, with baby powder and rotten fruit and coconut-smelling Jerri-Curl and shellac and cheap perfume. One beat-up wooden bench runs between the two rows of gray metal lockers to a windowless wall and the opening to the bathroom. On the mounted mirror, someone has written in permanent ink: What are you looking at, fat bitch? Above the mirror are the posters, the usual Harvey Edwards, one of Judith Jamison in *Cry,* the group shot from *Blues Suite,* the half-naked one of Bill T. Jones that makes my knees shake. And of course, on just about everything are the stickers reading Capezio with the tiny white stars poking out of a black background.

When I walk in, Caitlin turns away from me. I hear a faucet dripping, and her breathing. She yanks up her sweatshirt and pretends to get it stuck up over her head but I can tell she's rubbing her eyes. Maybe it's stupid, but seeing someone like her cry sort of scares me, and I forget all about being mad at her. I watch her slip off her tights, waiting for her to talk. She straddles the wooden bench, all varnished and grooved and etched with the names of hundreds of girls like us. She twists her arm up around her back and fumbles at the safety pin tucking the neckline of her ripped leotard under her bra strap. I could help her, but she doesn't ask, and so I let her grab at it until it flops open, stabbing her, and she curses and gives up. "Gimme a hand already, will you?" she says, and I sit down behind her and remove the pin. She reaches into her bag and pulls out a Newport, even though we're not allowed to smoke in the locker room, and so I know she's okay. She pulls her leotard down to her waist and unsnaps her bra, and I can see her bare back ripple with all that pumping iron when she sucks at the cigarette.

"I wanna go over to your house for a while, okay?"

I say, "Okay," which seems to make her feel better. She throws her leg around, faces me on the bench, and takes my hands and we play a clapping game, which ends up a game of scissor, paper, rock. "They're definitely fucking," she says, and, turning up a rock to my scissors, she whips me a vicious one then leans back on the bench laughing. Puffing her chest up in the air like a *Playboy* model with me as the photographer, she then extends her legs and squeezes my ears with her crusty, tape-wrapped feet, and I am frankly nervous.

"What are you doing?" I say, gulping. "Get off. Put your shirt on, whore!" She tosses back her thick, orangy mane, French-inhales, and in Julianna's squeaky, overpronouncing tone says, "Ooh, *Mer*edith! Oh, my baby, baby, how you tickle me so!"

And that's when we hear the scuffling in by the toilet stalls and know we're not alone. I snatch the Newport out of her hand, stamp it out on the bench, scramble for a can of hairspray in my bag, and spritz the room with its sugary scent. But Caitlin, stalking out bare-chested like Sheena of the Jungle, heads in toward the toilets and begins peeking under the stalls and fiddling with the latches. I scan the room, all cluttered with dance bags and clothes and food wrappers and butts. Then I notice the two open lockers. One is Caitlin's; and hanging over the corner of the other half-open door are Julianna's special-ordered pointe shoes from Freed's of London. Before I can run in there, I hear the thump of a forced-open stall door, a scared squeal, and Caitlin's chuckle. The moldy-green room reeks of bowl freshener, but no one ever turns on the fan since a couple of pigeons have shacked up in the vent. I step up behind Caitlin and crane my neck to look over her broad, bare shoulders. And there's Julianna, her ankles bound up by her tight jeans, sitting folded in on herself and wriggling, looking trapped like the frogs we had to pin onto those white wax lumps in Biology class. She has her glasses on now, and her eyes seem to take up half her face as she moves them from me to Caitlin and back. The only movement in the room is the drip of the faucet and the one ball of sweat that crawls through the spiky hairs on the back of Caitlin's neck, rolls up and down over her shoulder blades, down to the small of her back, soaking into the black cotton gathered there. I clear my throat, ready to tackle her, but she finally steps back into me and slams the door, making the whole row shake.

"Sorry," she calls. She turns and shrugs at me. "Didn't know anybody was in there."

Before we head to my house, I wash the smoke off my hands and face with the neon pink liquid from the soap dispensers (just in case my mom is home) and brush my teeth while Caitlin gets dressed. I try to hurry because as long as we're there, Julianna won't come out of the toilet stall for anything. After a while, I can't stand the silence. I say, "Julianna, your ankle looks like it's getting better, today." I'm not talking loud, but my voice bounces everywhere; it's stupid, but I feel like a Benedict Arnold for talking to her. After a second, her thin voice comes out, "It's better. Thanks." The words echo like she's inside the toilet bowl herself. Another pause, and she says, "You looked really good in the second movement today." My mouth is full of rinsing water when Caitlin comes in frowning and taps me.

"We're ready to go," she says.

I nod and spit. As I'm walking out, Caitlin says from behind me, "It stinks like dead fish in here," then flips the long-unused ventilation switch. There is a tired whir, a hum, then sounds of pigeons scrambling and a crackling like an axe through a wicker basket. I grab her and drag her outside fast.

The whole walk home, she refuses to say anything about what happened with her and Meredith. Instead, we have a mock argument. To get to my place, we have to walk past the house of the back-to-Africa group called Move; the TV calls it a "headquarters" but to me it just looks like a nasty old rundown stinky little *house*. I've lived in this part of West Philadelphia all my life and the neighborhood around here is actually pretty nice, but folks have had trouble here, and the house does smell funky on humid days like this, and so I go a little out of my way to walk on the opposite, upwind curb. Caitlin is babbling, talking about her solidarity with them, which of course comes from being cheated out by Julianna. I groan. One part of her tough act which drives me nuts is pretending she's poor and downtrodden; she tells people she's from "Uptown Manhattan" in a way that implies Harlem rather than her mom's fancy condo on Central Park West. She even carries around a little ki-Swahili phrase book with her and tries to teach me words, mostly as a joke, but today I'm not laughing.

"Let's go up there and ring the doorbell and run," she says, giggling. I grab her by the arm and drag her on. She can talk, with her own apartment and free lifestyle, dropped out of school, never having to work. She probably doesn't know what it's like to be made late for ballet classes, trapped in the schoolyard being pushed and taunted and called Oreo, called white. And as we turn the corner and approach my stoop, I'm slightly ashamed even though it's a nice, two-story house on a clean block. I'm ashamed, too, of my brother, Kevin, who's sitting on the step with the radio blaring, scanning Caitlin with bloodshot eyes made fat through his gazillion-dollar, thick-lensed Gazelles. He probably didn't go to summer school today; I see he's high on pot from the way he giggles and stands up to assume fifth position like a crippled stork, mocking me. I walk past and ignore him. I don't fail to notice that Caitlin's making eyes.

It's hot. We make sandwiches, make lemonade, and zone out with some TV. I'm hoping she'll tell me what happened in the office, but then dumb old Kevin comes in and plops his lazy butt on the couch next to her. Caitlin takes off her blouse, leaving only a cut-off half-tank top—a green color to match her eyes—matted to her torso with sweat.

"Kevin," I say, "the air conditioner is still broken."

He covers his mouth with his hand, goes, "Hmm," and looks away.

"The repairman was supposed to come today, right?"

"I don't know," Kevin says, looking at Caitlin, not me. "I wasn't here."

"Damn it, Kevin. You were supposed to come home right after school and let him in!"

"What are you, Mel, my mother?" he says, chuckling like a goon. Caitlin laughs, too.

If you live in this city during July without AC, you know all about the four-shower-a-day cure. It's irritating me, them making googly eyes on the couch, and it's so hot I decide to take a long, cold one. As I'm going up the stairs, I hear them giggling and think I hear a lighter flicking.

"Mom'll kill you, you smoke in here. Go on the stoop!" I say, then go up.

"What are you, his mother?" Caitlin yells. "Don't be in there all day, douche bag!"

Kevin's room is right across from the bathroom, and hanging on the door is a message board where he writes stuff like, "Don't wake me up," or "No, I didn't clean it yet." I scribble "Jerkoff" on it and have my shower.

I'm relaxing, forgetting about the day, playing with the shower massager and singing. It feels so good, easing my aching doggies with the loofah, I think I never want to get out. Then, after about thirty minutes, I hear the bathroom door creak open. I can't believe it. Through the plastic curtain, I see a shape, Caitlin's, naked and shiny, rounded and dark red-brown like a violin. I can also make out a taller, darker figure behind in the doorway. "Oh my God," I say, tearing aside the plastic, reaching for a towel to cover myself.

"What do you think you're doing?" I say, and I've a funny, knotted feeling inside. Before Caitlin finishes saying, "We're coming in with you, douche bag," I see Kevin, also naked, grinning, lurking there in the hall like some doorman. I look back at her, check out her bunchy, shining cheeks, and know what she calls a "just-fucked glow" when I see one.

"Oh no you don't!" I shout, yanking Caitlin in by her hard arm. Kevin scratches himself, raises a gangly arm, points to the ceiling like he's just hit on the answer to the theory of relativity, and goes, "Yo!"

"Get lost, Lurch!" I yell, slamming the door on his lousy grin. Livid, I shake Caitlin and beg, "Please tell me what you think you're doing here." Dripping wet as I am, she hugs me, and I smell pot smoke in her hair. Seeing my face above her shoulder in the mirror, I feel used. Without really thinking, I grab a hairbrush off the sink and smack her with it. Kevin tries to poke his head in again, and I hurl it at his chest, shouting, "Mom's gonna kill both of us, now!" I hear a slam across the hall and the rattle of the message-board pen.

Gripping Caitlin by the elbow, I swing the door open, make sure the way is clear, and drag her down the hall to my room. Still wet, I throw on my purple sweats and sandals, go back out, pound on Kevin's door until he throws out her clothes, and get her dressed. "I can't believe you," I keep saying over and over, although I actually can.

"I don't see why you're so uptight, girl," she complains. As I drag her back down the hall, she sings out, "Bye, Kevin." And from behind his door comes a muffled "Later." The living room reeks of pot, but I can't find the roach; Kevin usually eats them when he's done. I pick up her bag and blouse from the couch, dump them in her hands, and throw her outside onto the porch.

"Where we going?" she says, but I'm too choked up to answer.

I push her ahead of me down the street, back toward Philidance and the bus into Center City, past the stinky house. I'm thinking of things I want to say to her, but finally decide it's just time for her to go home. Halfway there, she tells me she's left her wallet in the locker at Philidance. My heart sinks. That means *I'll* have to go in; if Meredith saw Caitlin like this...

"I love you, Mel," she says, sounding pathetic, embarrassing me. "You know I love you."

"You shut up, Caitlin," I say, still choking. "You're just fucked up, that's all."

"You're angry," she says. Can you believe it? "It's all that lesbo white bitch's fault..."

"Are you crazy?!" I yell, unable to control myself. "Have you just lost your mind or something? It's not Julianna's fault, it's your fault! This whole day has been one big waste 'cause you go acting like a mental patient, walking around all slutty and half-naked thinking you're the Queen of Sheba, fucking my brother, terrorizing Julianna, mouthing off to everybody, getting me in trouble at rehearsal *and* at home..." She flinches as if I am hitting her, but sort of giggles, too, her eyes fixed on the *Cats* button on her bag. From my experiences with Kevin, I know the signs. "You know, girl," I say, "the only thing I love more than having fucked-up people telling me how they love me over and over again is having an argument with them when they're too stupid to get it. Look at you, all giggling and bobbing your head like one of those Moonies that can't speak English." She doesn't answer, so I just clamp my mouth shut, feeling ready to pop.

We turn the corner and tramp up the block back toward Philidance. She keeps looking all around like she's lost. I have to tug her by the sleeve. "Why don't we move to New York together, Mel? You and me."

"You shut up now, Caitlin."

As we come up opposite the red brick building, I glance into the diner to see if any teachers are there, but it's empty. I tell her to stay there and wait for me.

"I think I should get a cab," she says, staring into the sky. "I'm gonna get a cab."

"Whatever," I say.

"You gotta wait so long for a cab in Philadelphia," she whines, taking it as a personal insult.

"Whatever," I repeat. I check for traffic, then run across and up into the building. Usually, we have to knock on the door until Jimmy, the security guard, comes to let us in, but the front doors are still unlocked. I slip in—hallway's clear, office door's closed—and head to the locker room. After three tries, I remember the numbers on her combination lock and curse as mounds and mounds of junk tumble out at my feet. I go through the pile, nothing. I reach up over the top shelf, come out with a package of Twinkies, a Prince cassette without the box, a photo of Caitlin and some thirtyish-looking guy down at Penn's Landing, an autographed snapshot of Takako Asakawa, but no wallet. Then I see in the back a man's dance belt hanging from a hook like a trophy, and the black eelskin wallet nestled inside its crotch pouch. I kick the pile of junk back into the locker and dash out again.

In the hall, I rush past old Jimmy, who looks a lot like my granddad just before he died. He waves his rank cigar at me. As always, he shouts out in that gravelly, one-lunged voice, "Close dat do' behind you!"

"Okay, Jim!"

When I reach the front stoop, I see the yellow-checkered cab at the curb, with Caitlin and Julianna standing by the open rear door. Expecting the worst, I run down crazily going, "Hold it! Hold it!" Julianna stands with one arm crossed in front around her stomach, the other fluttering on her flat chest. She doesn't look too nervous, but she doesn't look too comfortable either. Caitlin, a good four inches shorter, stands with her legs apart, hands on hips, slightly rocking forward, staring at the hand like a drunk kitten watching a moth. Only the sweaty-faced, blond-bearded cabbie actually turns to look at me.

"What are you doing?" I demand, breathless.

Caitlin looks at me for a second and says, "Oh! Where did you go?" She lets out a whooping laugh, doing Moms Mabley again. "Me and Jules here just been patching things up 'tween us. Isn't that right, chile?" I look to Julianna, who crinkles up her freckly forehead and nods, but slides the hand up to her ear again. It occurs to me now that she may do this simply because of the *volume* of girls' talk at a place like Philidance; we get pretty loud compared to the backstage twitter at a place like the Pennsylvania Ballet. Caitlin is practically screaming in her ear, "Tell Mel how I 'pologized!"

"Sure," Julianna says, giving some twist of her cheek resembling a smile.

"That's right!" Caitlin bellows, beaming at me. I hand over her wallet and nod, but don't trust her for a second. "I even suggested we take this here cab together, didn't I? But we going in opposite directions, right?" She unsnaps the wallet, starts leafing intently through it, and answers herself, "That's right, Jules. Well, I feel soooo bad for giving you a hard time, a new girl like you. Tell you what, you take this cab." She walks around to the front passenger-side window and calls the cabbie to attention. "Hey, baby." Suddenly springing to life, he slaps the Obsession cologne dispenser on the dashboard and spins around. "Call up on that radio to get me another ride, okay? Make him a cutie, too." The man strokes his gold beard all sad, kissing his dream fare goodbye.

"You don't have to . . ." Julianna begins, but Caitlin halts her, throwing a hand up like a traffic cop.

"No, I feel so bad. I want you to. Guess I was just a little jealous, you know, with you being new and all. I guess I thought, was hoping, maybe me or Mel here shoulda had the part, but that's nothing. Best girl won, is all. Go on, take the cab." I feel my face take on an amazed expression that must make me look as stupid as Kevin. Caitlin bends to lean into the cab, and again I fixate on the bumps of her lower spine, like a dinosaur's, exposed when her half-top creeps up. The cabbie makes no effort to pretend he's not ogling the cleavage and round skin tumbled towards him, but only nods when she says, "Take gooood care of my girlfrien' here, baby! I'll find you if you don't. She gonna be a star someday!" She flashes a big, phony smile, puts her elbow up on the open rear doorframe and returns to her wallet-search, and I know now something is *definitely* wrong.

"Well, okay. Thank you," says Julianna. She hesitates, then holds out a hand to shake, but Caitlin is too wrapped up in digging through her wallet, so she throws her bag in across the seat. "Thank you very much, Caitlin." Ducking her head, bending with difficulty in those skintight jeans, Julianna scoots butt-forward halfway into the cab. At that moment, Caitlin lets out a chilling whoop and swings on me; puffing her cheeks and squinting her eyes, she shouts, "Where's my money, witch?!"

"What?" I am staggered.

"I trust you to get my wallet 'cause I'm not feeling well, and you go and rip me off like this? How was I supposed to get home? You think of that?!"

I'm wondering, What the hell is she talking about? First, I'm thinking, I got the wrong wallet. Then I'm thinking, Maybe she just wants an excuse to make Julianna have to share a ride. Pulling me into some kind of game. I try to nip it in the bud. "I got money, Caitlin," I say. "You'll get home."

But she just twists up her face uglier, meaner, steps into me chest-to-chest, hisses, "Damn right I will! Gimme my fucking money, nigger!" I'm so floored I can't talk, can't move, just let her push me back a step. I'm thinking, Or maybe Julianna ripped her off out of revenge? In the corner of my eye, I see the pale girl paralyzed, frozen one leg in, one leg out of the cab, not knowing what to do—to help me or not. I know she didn't do it.

"You gonna get yours!" Caitlin howls, jumping at me. She gets me in a clench, popping me in the sides with rabbit punches, but not hard enough to hurt. I'm wondering, What the fuck...? And then, just as I'm giving her the lightest of shoves, I see her grin.

I can swear I hardly *touched* her. But that's not what makes me guilty. My memory sees it like a slow-mo replay of a pole vaulter—mouth open, sharp shoulder first—but really it took less than a blink. Even though I didn't know what was going on, I sort of did. This cloudy, fleeting thought zapped out of my head like a piece of burnt toast popping out of a toaster too late. Big break, are the words I thought. Julianna didn't have time to move.

Under her own force, I'm sure—off those legs that could press two hundred pounds easy—Caitlin hurls back through the air wearing a big Cheshire grin. That muscular back meets the window glass, that ass hardened by a hundred hours bent over in ancient African dance poses blots out the yellow and black checkers of the door. There's a white flash of sun off the chrome handle. I see the blue denim and the crisscross laces on the white girl's bare, freckled ankle. I see her sandal sole still glued to the melting black street tar, then rust on the yellow metal edge of the door. A crunch like a heavy suitcase slamming bounces down the steamy, empty street. The cabbie only shuts his eyes and throttles his beard. And I hear the howl floating up and up like a ghost mixed with the flapping and squawking of the pigeons which scatter from the sidewalk and zip out of sight over the roof of the dance school.

That's how my name got into that program.

When I came back out of the office from calling 911, the sun still hung there high and hot, but tired. The cabbie stood a foot or two from the car, trying to decide whether to keep his hands in or out of his pockets, finally settling on stroking and sniffing his beard. He had removed his shirt—to wrap the leg, I suppose—and I saw a tattoo of a skeleton holding up a banner reading *Baby-doll* on his shoulder, and rings of clumped, soggy powder under his armpits. I saw the clotted red-brown like barbecue sauce already baking into the nooks of the tar. I didn't look inside the taxi. Obviously, Caitlin was nowhere to be seen.

I missed her call the next day, as Meredith was forced to hold a string of emergency rehearsals with me and a new group of girls, but I had already figured she was on her way back to New York. Walking in that Sunday morning, I stopped at the diner and got a coffee in an "I Love Philly" paper cup and a pack of Newports from the machine. Then, I went straight in, was asked by my reflection, "What are you looking at, fat bitch," dialed the combination by memory, and moved into her locker.

I got the solo. After I told some parts of this story to Meredith a couple of times, she said that I had been doing much better, though not in the way you'd say it to a big fish. Like I said, I'm an okay dancer, and there are lots of girls trying to do this who are less than okay, especially in the summer months when the first company is away touring or on vacation. It wasn't a great show, but it ran for a week and people liked it. I was pleased by the applause, and people came up afterward and smeared lipstick on my face and told me I was fierce and that made me feel good. My mom and dad brought flowers, and they forced Kevin to sit through it, too. I even got a write-up in two little weekend tabloids; one of them even called me "graceful."

But like I said, it's a hard business. Since that time, I've only performed in one big jazz piece—shoved way in the background, as jazz is sexier and only works with women's bodies. It's okay, though, since I'm mostly occupied now preparing to take the PSATs for college. My favorite thing still is coming in alone on a weekend, closing the door politely for old Jimmy, reading that sign by the front,

> *Those who dance are thought mad*
> *by those who hear not the music.*

Stirring up the rosin dust on the sprung floors with my eyes closed, sleepwalking, trusting I'll sort it all out later, I just figure that right now I've got all the moments in the sun I need.

CONTRIBUTORS' NOTES

Ploughshares · Spring 1993

PAULETTE BATES ALDEN is the author of a collection of short stories, *Feeding the Eagles* (Graywolf Press). She has recently completed a book-length memoir, *A Reluctant Education*, another excerpt of which appeared in *The New York Times Magazine*. She is currently a Benedict Distinguished Visiting Professor at Carleton College in Northfield, Minn. **JAN BAILEY** is this year's South Carolina Arts Commission Poetry Fellow. Her poems have appeared most recently in *Prairie Schooner, The Greensboro Review, Mudfish,* and *Willow Springs*. Bailey, who earned an M.F.A. from Vermont College, has completed a first manuscript, *The Healing Street*. She divides her time between South Carolina and Monhegan Island, Maine. **DINAH BERLAND**'s poetry has appeared or is forthcoming in *The Iowa Review, New Letters, Hayden's Ferry Review, Yellow Silk, Pearl,* and elsewhere. Formerly an art critic and photographer, Berland currently works as a free-lance book editor and lives in an original Victorian house in downtown Los Angeles. **CYRUS CASSELLS** is the author of two books of poetry, *The Mud Actor* (Holt), which was a 1982 National Poetry Series selection and nominee for the Bay Area Book Reviewers Award, and the forthcoming *Soul Make a Path Through Shouting* (Copper Canyon Press, 1994). He received the 1992 Peter I. B. Lavan Younger Poet Award, given by the Academy of American Poets. **MARY CLARK**'s poems have appeared in *The Iowa Review, Black Warrior Review, Passages North,* and *River Styx*. She also has a story in the current issue of *Fiction*. **SHEP CLYMAN** received his M.A. from New York University in May 1992. He has taught at NYU and at Goldwater Hospital. He does not have a dog, but his roommate has a cat who avoids him. **JANET COLEMAN** is the author of *The Compass: The Improvisational Theatre That Revolutionized American Comedy* (Knopf/Univ. of Chicago Press) and co-author with Al Young of *Mingus/Mingus: Two Memoirs* (Creative Arts/Limelight). Recently she has written for *Esquire, Elle, Instant Classics III,* and *The Bloomsbury Review*. She is the voice of Emily Ann Andrews on the radio series *Poisoned Arts*. **SAM CORNISH**'s books include *Songs of Jubilee, Generations, 1935: A Memoir,* and *Folks Like Me,* a new collection of poems that has just been released by Zoland Books. He was born in Baltimore, Md., and now lives in Brighton, Mass. The former Literature Director for the Massachusetts Council on the Arts and Humanities, Cornish teaches literature and minority studies at Emerson College. **RUSSELL SUSUMU ENDO** is a Japanese-American poet. He has had poems published in *The American Poetry Review, Hawaii Pacific Review, Hawaii Review,* and elsewhere. His poem "Susumu, My Name" was incorporated by Sumi Tonooka into a jazz orchestra piece. **MARTÍN ESPADA** was awarded the PEN/Revson Foundation Fellowship, as well as the Paterson Poetry

Prize, for his most recent collection of poems, *Rebellion Is the Circle of a Lover's Hands* (Curbstone, 1990). His next book, *City of Coughing and Dead Radiators*, is forthcoming from W.W. Norton in 1993. **CAROLYN FERRELL** has lived, worked, and studied in West Berlin, Manhattan, and the South Bronx. Her stories have appeared in *The Literary Review, Callaloo, Fiction,* and *Sojourner: The Women's Forum.* She is currently working on a collection of short stories and teaches at Lehman College in the Bronx. **SUSAN JANE GILMAN** currently attends the M.F.A. creative writing program at the University of Michigan, where she has received two Hopwood Awards for fiction and a Cowden Memorial Fellowship. Her work has appeared in *The New York Times, Newsday,* and *The Village Voice,* among other publications. **GABRIELLE GLANCY** teaches writing at the New College of California. Her work has appeared in *The Paris Review, The American Poetry Review, The Kenyon Review, Ploughshares, Agni,* and *New American Writing.* She has been the recipient of several awards, including a New York Foundation for the Arts Fellowship and the Malinche Prize for her translation of a Marguerite Duras book. She is currently translating a book by Jean Genet. **MICHELE GLAZER** lives in Portland, Oreg. **JOSHUA HENKIN** is an M.F.A. student at the University of Michigan and winner of a 1992 PEN Syndicated Fiction Award. His stories have appeared or are forthcoming in *The Massachusetts Review, Cimarron Review, The Seattle Review,* and *The Southern Review,* and have been nominated for the Pushcart Prize. He is at work on a novel. **STEPHEN HENRIQUES** recently had a one-man show in San Francisco and has exhibited nationwide. The cover painting, *Habana Noche* (61 " x 60 "), is from one of his series of jazz paintings. He lives and works in San Francisco. **JANE HIRSHFIELD**'s most recent books are *Of Gravity & Angels* (Wesleyan, 1988) and a co-translation, *The Ink Dark Moon* (Vintage, 1990). In 1994, HarperCollins will publish *The October Palace.* Her work appears in *The Atlantic, The American Poetry Review, The Paris Review,* and elsewhere. **JAMES D. HOUSTON** has written six novels, including *Continental Drift* and *Love Life,* both from Knopf. His stories and essays appear this year in *The True Subject* (Graywolf), *The Sound of Writing 2* (Doubleday/Anchor), and *Dreamers and Desperadoes: Contemporary Fiction from the American West* (Dell). He lives in Santa Cruz, Calif. **STEWART DAVID IKEDA**, 26, is a free-lance writer and editor of several publications at the University of Michigan, where he earned his M.F.A. and won two Hopwood Awards: one for a novel-in-progress and another for a story collection. His poetry and prose have received awards from NYU, the Kentucky State Poetry Society, and New York City's *A Different Drummer.* A story of his will appear in the May issue of *Glimmer Train.* **COLETTE INEZ** is the author of five poetry collections, and has received fellowships from the Guggenheim and Rockefeller foundations and twice from the NEA. She has taught poetry at Ohio University, Bucknell, Kalamazoo College, and the New School, and is currently on the faculty of Columbia University's Writing Program. Her *New & Selected Poems* is due out from Story Line Press this spring. **STACEY LAND JOHNSON** teaches a poetry class at the University of Arizona. Her work also appears in *Grand Street.* **JIM KUPECZ** is a fifty-two-year-old, blue-collar worker who lives in Rochester, N.Y. In addition to fiction, essays, and theater pieces, he generally writes long, discursive poems which explore the boundary between formal and colloquial language. This is the first time his work has appeared in print outside of New York State. SUSAN LUDVIGSON is Poet-in-Residence and Professor of English at Winthrop University in South Carolina. Her most recent book of poems is *To Find the Gold* (LSU Press, 1990). In the fall, LSU will publish her new collection, *Everything Winged Must Be Dreaming.* DAVID MAMET is the author of the plays *American Buffalo, Sexual Perversity in Chicago, Speed the Plow, Glengarry Glen Ross* (for which he won a Pulitzer Prize), and *Oleanna,* which is currently an off-Broadway hit. He also wrote and directed the films *Homicide, House of Games,* and *Things Change,* and was the screenwriter for *The Untouchables* and *Hoffa.* He recently published a collection of essays with Turtle Bay Books entitled *The Cabin.* MORTON MARCUS has published six books of poetry, the most recent of which is *Pages From a Scrapbook of Immigrants* (Coffee House Press, 1988). In 1992, Capitola Book Company reissued his book *Santa Cruz Mountain Poems.* Marcus, whose poems have appeared in more than fifty anthologies, teaches at Cabrillo College. JACK MARSHALL is the author of *Arriving on the Playing Fields of Paradise,* which won the 1983 Bay Area Book Reviewers Award. *Arabian Nights,* his most recent collection of poetry, was published in 1987 by Coffee House Press, which will also be publishing his next volume, *Sesame,* in the fall. COLLEEN J. MCELROY has been the recipient of the Before Columbus American Book Award, two Fulbrights, two NEA Fellowships, and a Rockefeller Fellowship. Her most recent books are *Driving Under the Cardboard Pines,* a collection of fiction, and *What Madness Brought Me Here: New and Selected Poems, 1968–88.* McElroy also writes for the stage and television, and her work has been translated into Russian, Italian, German, Malay and Serbo-Croatian. She lives in Seattle, Wash. MARTIN MCKINSEY's "The Luminosity of Sheets" is one of several longer narratives in his new manuscript, *Inland Sea.* He has translated extensively from modern Greek, including Vassilis Tsiamboussis's story "A Pat on the Cheek," which appeared in the Fall 1992 issue of *Ploughshares.* SHEILA J. PACKA is a poet and social worker living in Duluth, Minn. She received a Loft McKnight Award for Poetry in 1986 and a Loft Mentor Award in 1992. Her work has appeared in *Sing Heavenly Muse, Loonfeather,* and *Hurricane Alice,* and is forthcoming in *Sinister Wisdom, Rag Mag,* and *North Coast Review.* DIXIE PARTRIDGE has recent work in *Berkeley Poetry Review, Commonweal, Hollins Critic, Northern Lights, Passages North,* and *Southern Poetry Review,* among other publications. Her first book, *Deer in the Haystacks,* was published by Ahsahta Press in 1984. Her second, *Watermark,* won the 1990 Eileen W. Barnes Award and was issued by Saturday Press in 1991. CARL PHILLIPS's first book, *In the Blood* (Northeastern Univ. Press, 1992), was selected by Rachel Hadas for the Samuel French Morse Poetry Prize. The George Starbuck Fellow in poetry at Boston University this year, he has work forthcoming in *Agni, Indiana Review, Chelsea,* and *Witness.* JACK RIDL has published two collections of poetry: *The Same Ghost* and *Between,* both from Dawn Valley Press. He is finishing a third volume, *Losing Season,* which includes the poems in this issue. Ridl grew up with basketball. His father is the former head coach at Westminster College and the University of Pittsburgh. FRANK RUSSELL has returned to Florida after five years of teaching at Fisk University. His first full-length collection, *Dinner With Dr. Rocksteady,* was published by Ion Books/Raccoon in 1987, and his poems have appeared in *Poetry, Chelsea, Poetry Northwest, New Letters, Raccoon, The Chariton Review, Porch, Southern Poetry Review,* and *The Kansas Quarterly.* He will begin serving as a Peace Corps Teacher-Trainer in Poland in June. NATASHA SAJE is a Ph.D. candidate at the University of Maryland, where she is writing a study entitled *"Artful Artlessness": Reading the Coquette in the American Novel.* She has recent or forthcoming poems in *Antaeus, Chelsea, Poetry,* and elsewhere. PETER SCHMITT's collection of poems, *Country Airport,* was published by Copper Beech Press. He has received the Peter I. B. Lavan Younger Poet Award from the Academy of American Poets and the "Discovery"/*The Nation* Prize for Poetry. He has recent work in *The Paris Review* and *The Southern Review,* and poems forthcoming in *Poetry.* JAMES SCOFIELD is a poet living and writing in Olympia, Wash. L. E. SCOTT is from Brimfield, Ohio, and her work has appeared in recent issues of *Hayden's Ferry Review, The Oyez Review, The Old Red Kimono, NRG,* and *Hurricane Alice.* She is currently completing an M.F.A. at George Mason University in Fairfax, Va. PEGGY SHUMAKER has two collections of poems due out in 1993: a full-length book from the Pitt Poetry Series and a letterpress chapbook, *Braided River,* from Limner Press in Anchorage. Her work was included in *The Pittsburgh Book of Contemporary American Poetry* and in *From the Republic of Conscience,* an anthology benefiting Amnesty International. She teaches in the M.F.A. program at the University of Alaska, Fairbanks, and is president of the board of Associated Writing Programs. ANN SNODGRASS's poems have appeared in *The Paris Review, The Partisan Review, The American Poetry Review,* and *Agni,* among other publications. She currently lives in the Netherlands, where she teaches writing and literature at Emerson College's campus in Maastricht. TERESE SVOBODA's most recent book, *Laughing Africa,* shared the Iowa Prize in 1990. Last fall, she was a Distinguished Visiting Professor at the University of Hawaii, and this spring she co-curated *Word and Image* for the Museum of Modern Art in New York City. PATRICK SYLVAIN was born in Port-au-Prince, Haiti, and emigrated to Massachusetts in 1981. He works as a bilingual public schoolteacher in Cambridge, while pursuing an M.A. in Education and American Civilization. Sylvain, who is a member of the Dark Room Collective, has published work in *African American Review, Agni, American Poetry Anthology, Haiti Progress, Moody Street Review, Muleteeth, Prisma,* and *In the Tradition: An Anthology of Young Black Writers.* RICHARD TILLINGHAST has published poems recently in *The Atlantic Monthly, The New Yorker, The Best American Poetry 1992, The Paris Review,* and *The Hudson Review.* His fifth book, *The Stonecutter's Hand,* will be published by David R. Godine in 1994. For the past ten years, he has taught at the University of Michigan. NANCE VAN WINCKEL teaches in

Eastern Washington University's M.F.A. Program and edits *Willow Springs*. She is the author of *Bad Girl, With Hawk* (Univ. of Illinois Press, 1988), and has recent poems in *The American Poetry Review, The Denver Quarterly, The Antioch Review, Shenandoah,* and *New England Review.* She has a collection of stories forthcoming from the University of Missouri Press. REX WILDER is Director of the Poetry Society of America in Los Angeles. His work has appeared or is forthcoming in *The Nation, Poetry, The Georgia Review, The Antioch Review,* and *The Southwest Review,* among others. JEROME WILSON lives in Memphis, Tenn. He wrote "Paper Garden" in the P&H Café in February 1993. He has completed a collection of short stories, and is currently at work on his first novel. GINGER WINEINGER is a free-lance editor living in Jersey City, N.J. Her fiction has appeared in *Yellow Silk* and is forthcoming in *Cottonwood.* She has begun work on a new novel, *Slip Tracing.* RODNEY WITTWER has published poems in *The Antioch Review, The Madison Review,* and other journals, and has work forthcoming in *Hayden's Ferry Review.* He lives in West Medford, Mass. KEVIN YOUNG attended Harvard University, where he received the Academy of American Poets Prize in 1989. He is a member of the Dark Room Collective and co-founder of Fisted Pick Press, both Boston-based efforts devoted to emerging and established black writers. Currently he is a Stegner Poetry Fellow at Stanford University. His work has appeared or is forthcoming in *Agni, Callaloo, The Kenyon Review,* and *Graham House Review.* The poems in this issue are taken from his first manuscript, *Most Way Home.* RAY A. YOUNG BEAR is a lifetime resident of the Mesquakie (Red Earth) Tribal Settlement in central Iowa. His poems have appeared in *The American Poetry Review, TriQuarterly, The Georgia Review, The Kenyon Review,* and *Harper's Anthology of 20th Century Native American Poetry,* among other publications. His books include *Winter of the Salamander* (Harper & Row), *The Invisible Musician* (Holy Cow! Press), and *Black Eagle Child: The Facepaint Narratives* (Univ. of Iowa Press). He is currently at work on a nonfiction book, *Stories From the Woodland Region,* and a collection of poems, *The Rock Island Hiking Club.*

ABOUT AL YOUNG

Ploughshares · Spring 1993

What strikes you first about Al Young is the voice. It's a dee-jay's voice—articulate; engaging; most of all, *smooth*—so it's not surprising to find out that for several years, Young hosted jazz shows in Detroit for WDET and in Berkeley for KJAZ, work-ed as a public radio announcer, and performed as an actor on educational radio productions. Music and the spoken word, or "platters and chatter," as they called it in the Fifties, have been abiding influences in Young's life and in his prolific career as a writer. His books include the poetry collections *Dancing, The Song Turning Back Into Itself, Geography of the Near Past, The Blues Don't Change: New and Selected Poems,* and *Heaven: Collect-ed Poems 1956–1990;* the novels *Snakes, Who Is Angelina?, Sitting Pretty, Ask Me Now,* and *Seduction by Light;* and three "musical memoirs," *Bodies & Soul, Kinds of Blue,* and *Things Ain't What They Used to Be.* He has also written numerous screenplays, such as *Bustin' Loose* for Richard Pryor, and edited anthologies and the literary journals *Loveletter* and, with Ishmael Reed, *The Yardbird Reader* and *Quilt.*

Born in 1939 in Ocean Springs, Mississippi, Young was raised first in Mississippi and then in Detroit, and the contrasts between North and South, the city and country, strongly contributed to his curiosity about the world at large, the mystery of what he could not see. As a child, he and his family would walk down to the Gulf of Mexico nearly every day to get shrimp and crabs, and he remembers being intrigued by the ocean and the boats, "the fact that there was a *beyond.*" To bridge the distances, he lis-tened—listened to stories told by his family on the front porch and to music and to the old radio shows, fascinated by every pro-gram, even—much to his grandmother's amusement—Arthur Godfrey's. When Young was a little older, he lived across the Detroit River from Windsor, Ontario, and he tuned into the Canadian Broadcasting Company, which aired jazz, pop, live symphony, plays, documentaries, and, seminally for him, poets like Dylan Thomas reading their works aloud. He was already somewhat familiar with poetry—his second-grade teacher, Mrs. Chapman, had made the class memorize and recite poems every two weeks—but this was different: "All the energy and little nuances and secret meanings and things that the voice transmits and conveys, I could hear all that for the first time. It came *alive* for me." He knew then that it was his destiny to become a poet, and he began, systematically, to go through the poetry shelves of the Detroit Public Library. An insatiable reader since the age of three, Young admits that the worst thing you can do is ask him to narrow down his favorite poets, but he points to Kenneth Patchen and Li Po as two who impressed him early on. Then he mentions Federico García Lorca, early T. S. Eliot, Rabinadrath Tagore, Vladimir Mayakovsky, Leopold Senghor, Blaise Cendrars, the Bible, Nicolás Guillén, Nicanor Parra, LeRoi Jones, Levertov, Coleridge, Keats, Shelley, Dickinson, Whitman...

In his teens, he began publishing poems, stories, and articles. He entered the University of Michigan at Ann Arbor with the intention of being a literature major, but was immediately discouraged. New Criticism reigned over English departments in those days, and the heavily structured approach took the fun out of it for Young. "I intuitively sensed that that kind of immersion was destructive to the creative urge." Such was his disappointment, he momentarily considered switching directions and becoming a lawyer, as his mother had suggested, since he had "the gift of gab." (Before she died, she told Young she was glad he had not become an attorney. When asked why, she said, "Because lawyers are liars. I wouldn't want a child of mine lying professionally. It's bad enough that writing these books, you use your imagination to the fullest.") What saved Young was a graduate-level seminar on Cervantes he was able to enroll in, although he was only a freshman. The professor, Sanchez Escribano, integrated the whole of Western culture and history into the study of *Don Quixote,* and Young thought, "This is it! This is what college is supposed to be—kicking back, the deep talking to the deep." At the start of his senior year, however, restlessness overtook him again, and he dropped out. He didn't think he needed a degree to

PHOTO: CAROLYN CLEBSCH

be a writer, and he believed traveling and supporting himself with odd jobs would be more edifying. Other than deejaying, he worked stints as a medical photographer, warehouseman, clerk-typist, interviewer for the California Department of Employment, yard clerk for the Southern Pacific Railroad, lab aide, industrial films narrator, and, with some prominence, singer and guitarist. "I did blues tunes, traditional folk fare," he recalls, "but I would put a little spin on it. Quite often I'd use jazz voicings or inject contemporary idioms." Yet ultimately, he rejected music as a career. Many years later, Young and his father, who had also been a professional musician, discussed why each had quit playing. "He was a teetotaler," Young says. "He saw his friends getting high and getting killed. Somebody would stab them, or they'd stab somebody and somebody would shoot them—all that stuff we think of as the colorful jazz life—and my father thought it was a waste. My version of it was that I literally got tired of going to the gigs. I hated that you had to *be* there. It was a drag. You had to put up with drunks and people saying, 'Play "Melancholy Baby." ' "

An astrologer once told Young that he was a classic Gemini, with two strong attributes: one part of him being very public and social, even a performer; the other side private, very solitary and reflective. He decided to pursue his quieter inclinations, and his plan was to go back to school, get his degree at Berkeley, and, for a living, teach Spanish—which he had studied since the seventh grade—while writing on the side. Remembering his experience at Ann Arbor, he wanted to avoid teaching literature and creative writing at all costs.

Ironically, he was hired as a writing instructor immediately upon graduation, and over the years he has taught creative writing at the University of California campuses of Santa Cruz and Berkeley, the University of Michigan, and the University of Washington. In addition, he has been a Jones Lecturer at Stanford and a Mellon Distinguished Professor of Humanities at Rice University. To this day, he has never conducted a single class in Spanish.

But mainly, of course, he has been writing, interested in how people find everyday worth and love in a technological world that is increasingly impersonal, trying to answer "those big questions that most people leave behind unless they go to divinity school or into ontology: Why the hell are we here? What's the meaning of it?" In his poetry, he tends to concentrate on a single image or issue, "looking at it from the most arbitrary of angles to see if it makes sense." In his novels, he reaches for a broader picture, seeing "how people go through a particular set of circumstances over a course of time and come out transformed or untransformed." And in his musical memoirs, which are collections of autobiographical essays and vignettes, all touched off by associations to songs, he feels the most freedom—a liberation he likens to Charlie Parker's experience in the early 1940s, when he made a recording of Ray Noble's "Cherokee": "He said he found out that by playing along the higher intervals of the chord changes to 'Cherokee,' he broke into a completely different range of dimension. He could play what he had been hearing in his head but hadn't figured out how to do on his horn. I feel the same thing when I'm writing about a particular song. I'm not limited by character or plot, and something happens. I can get into a lot of those deeper meanings."

Oddly, Young's versatility has sometimes worked against him.

Derek Walcott once inscribed a book: "For Al Young, the poet, with sympathy." Young asked what he meant. "Well," Walcott said, "I feel sorry for you, because in the United States, they like you to do one thing. What they don't notice is that whatever you do, you're a poet, you bring that poetic sensibility to it." There have been other criticisms as well, racial expectations and censures from all quarters, ranging from complaints that his prose style was not experimental and reactionary enough to accusations that he was bourgeois, especially in his musings about the African-American middle class, as if such people did not exist. He parodied the reproaches in a poem called "Your Basic Black Poet": "Why are there oceans in / his poems, sunshine, glacial / journeys toward reunion? / What's the matter with / his diction man he / sho dont sound black? / / Any way you look at it / the dude is irrelevant, / & dangerous to the community."

The pressure on him became so great, and so ludicrous, Young invented an alter ego, O. O. Gabugah, deriving the name from the South African poet Hugh Masakele's album *The Americanization of Oogabugah.* (Growing up in Johannesburg, Masakele watched *Tarzan* movies, heard "natives" uttering phrases like "Oogabugah, bowa masa," and for a while, actually thought that somewhere in Africa, people spoke that way.) "Fraudulent militant black poetry was starting to leak into the public province," Young says. "There was a legitimate form of social protest, people genuinely writing from their hearts and their guts and their minds for social change, addressing real injustice. And then you had people doing it or trying to exploit it because it was fashionable. The same sort of situation exists today with gangster rap, which has come to be largely consumed by suburban kids, rather than in the inner city, where it's passé. In the early Seventies, black anger was radical-chic and being successfully marketed to whites, and I thought it was time to do what Cervantes had done with the novel of chivalry; that is, poke a little fun at it. I caught hell for it. People liked O. O. Gabugah's poetry, but they didn't know what to make of him. They'd start applauding, and then they'd say, 'Wait a minute, wait a minute. Are you making fun of the Revolution? What the fuck is that supposed to mean?'" Young recounts teaching at Stanford during that period and discovering that his African-American students, who had been, for the most part, brought up in affluence, were all presenting "rat-and-roach" stories in workshops: "I would ask, 'Have you ever personally experienced the ghetto?' And they'd say, 'No, not personally, but I'm trying to relate to the brothers and sisters.' And I'd say, 'Well, why don't you write about growing up in Connecticut, or going to a fancy prep school as a black person, because I know the pain got to you there, too.'"

Throughout his career, Young has been more interested in how much people have in common, rather than how much they differ, and because of this, controversy always seems to follow him, a fact that is sometimes tiresome, but one that does not entirely displease him. Young—who devotes about six months of the year to his own writing in his Bay Area home, accepting one-semester contracts as a visiting professor and traveling across the country or overseas, giving readings, the rest of the time—is working on a new novel called *A Piece of Cake,* a sequel to *Sitting Pretty.* The main character, Sidney J. Prettymon, who is now in his seventies, wins the lottery. "All of my political detractors can get ready," Young warns with glee. "I'm fifty-three years old, I'm not making a fortune in this business, I can say whatever I want to say. In this one, I'm going for broke."

—Don Lee

FOLKS LIKE ME *Poems by Sam Cornish. Zoland Books, $12.95 cloth.*
Reviewed by Sven Birkerts.

Sam Cornish has written a book that subtly defies the norms.
This is not a gathering of "poems," or a showcase for isolated
tours de force, but rather an ambitious vocal collage in which
each poem is a voice and a stance toward the world, with each
voice then modifying or refuting the others. More ambitious still
is the scope of the undertaking. The "folks like me" of the title
are African Americans of all descriptions—working people,
entertainers, disaffected radicals, sober churchgoing folk—and
they step forth one after the other from the decades of our century to present their testimony. We hear the Depression-era sen-
timents of the unidentified speaker of the title poem: "In the
unemployment line / with those early morning / economic blues /
at home / on my feet   the president / said the economy is doing
fine / (guess it's just taking its time getting / down   to folks
like me)."

Cornish is, of course, playing off the old tune "Got Those Early
Monday Morning Workin' Blues..." Then, on the very next page,
in "What Can (Blind) Lemon Do?," he draws on the blues lexicon
to celebrate Blind Lemon Jefferson, who: "cocky in his Stetson
hat / said / (me & my guitar / makes ev'rything all / right) a fat
man / picking / for my liquor / my women (fine meat shaking / on
the bone) / on the sidewalks / my guitar and me."

But this is a sliver. The hundred-plus poems—many short,
most terse if not downright repressed in their diction—finally
give the reader the impression of a great force held strictly in
abeyance. This is the other part of Cornish's defiance. He refuses
the easy path, refuses to release his people into song. Their voices
are, by and large, determinedly restrained. "Negro Communist,"
for instance, reads like this in its entirety: "When white / workers
find / hotel rooms / the Negro worker / hits the street." End stop.

You stand there with the telegram and search for subtext. If you are black, you know; if you are part of the white culture, the message may or may not dawn on you. After a hundred telegrams it does.

It is only when Cornish introduces the voice of John, identified in the Glossary as "Personal friend who lived in Baltimore, and reflected a common attitude toward the sit-ins and bus boycotts," that we get the rage we might have expected sooner: "Thinking with his M-1 (red meat / lives in this nigger / body) / instead of the bar / the bottle / the hip / black world / or thinking / NAACP Negroes / this is me   my gun" (from "Homegrown Nigger #1"). But rage is not the last word, either. After the poems of the Sixties and Seventies, which refer to the Black Panthers, the Move bombings, and such, Cornish concludes with quiet celebrations of James Baldwin and poet Robert Hayden. Hayden, it seems, did not lend his voice to the cause of those who cried "burn / baby burn," but as the last lines of the book affirm, "it is Hayden's star / burning / now." Cornish has compacted a world in these pages. Read slowly, give his people their elbow room, and let the undertones gather into music.

Sven Birkerts is the author of three books of essays, An Artificial Wilderness, The Electric Life, *and* American Energies. *He has edited a new anthology,* Literature: The Evolving Canon, *which has just been published by Allyn and Bacon.*

THE WORLD BOOK *Poems by Steven Cramer. Copper Beech Press, $9.95 paper. Reviewed by H. L. Hix.*

"Sentimentality," Wallace Stevens said, "is a failure of feeling." The poems in Steven Cramer's courageous and powerful second collection, *The World Book,* risk that failure: they address themes susceptible to sentiment, such as the narrator's adolescence, the deaths of his father and brother, and his mother's illness; and they speak in the first person, the voice to which sentiment comes most easily. But Cramer's poems fight sentiment with our only available weapons: knowledge and integrity. His work recognizes and confronts the stupidity of adolescence, the ambiguity of political action, the facelessness of death, and the selfishness of grief. And ultimately, the poems, rather than succumbing to sentimentality, achieve intimacy.

Not even the narrator himself is sentimentalized. In "The Parade, 1968," he is one of a group of "three high school juniors / And a 4-F dropout" who protest the war by carrying a pasteboard casket with a "mirror for a face / Through the Brookside Independence / Day Parade." But no self-righteous posing poisons this poem: Cramer sees that the kids are motivated as much by fear and ignorance as by virtue, and that the girl "Who snatched our peace leaflets / And shredded them one by one" is motivated as much by grief as by patriotism, having recently "lost / Her brother's forearm to Khesanh." The poem ends with the protesters "cast adrift / With the floats and majorettes" at the end of the parade, left "To think *Now what?*," and able to find no answer more effective than to stand the casket on end so that it "Towered over us and them, / A head or more too tall / To reflect on anyone."

In "After Bypass," the narrator is in the hospital room with his recuperating mother: "Fresh from surgery, your sewn-up chest / Almost glowed through the sheer nightgown, / Its embossed ridge of stitches curving down / Between your breasts. What son could resist / A furtive look?" More than one otherwise competent poet has foundered on a mother's-breasts poem, "driven," to borrow George Oppen's words, "into sentimentality, having nowhere else to go"; but Cramer, through precise language, transforms that furtive look from voyeurism to self-scrutiny: inversion of subject and object reveals that they "left *me* exposed to *you*" (my italics).

The father's death is the most frequent subject of these poems, and Cramer faces it, too, with a hard-earned clarity. In a fine sonnet, the father and mother are shown at the moment when she is trying to give him a nitroglycerine pill, as they negotiate a "truce": "In a voice more like a mother's than a wife's, / *For me,* she pleads. He permits her to save his life." Cramer has not let grief make him forget that our need to be loved makes us selfish in our own death, and our fear of abandonment makes us selfish in the deaths of those we love. In "Constellations," the father himself has the sharpness of vision only experience combined with awareness of mortality can give. Watching stars and the lights of landing airplanes with his family, he forestalls the romanticizing of a shooting star by explaining that "they're only meteors, / Space debris so infinitesimal / Thousands could fit in his palm," and seeing at the same time his own star "Flame-out in the upper atmosphere, / A split-second of light / No one's quick enough to share."

In *The World Book*, Steven Cramer sets out to write "a narrative / Of everyone alive who now is not." That narrative's success results from Cramer's knowledge that "the punishing exactitude of memory" is the "single way to enter / Such cold water."

H. L. Hix teaches philosophy at the Kansas City Art Institute and has poems in the current issues of The Georgia Review, Northwest Review, *and* Four Quarters.

GOOD HOPE ROAD *Poems by Stuart Dischell. Viking, $20.00 cloth. Reviewed by Joyce Peseroff.*

While fretting over "environmental destruction," an old man faces his own mortality. A woman waiting for a tow truck wishes she were older or younger, "that what she had been / Waiting for all her life would finally begin to happen." A supermarket manager resists broadcasting family problems "as if he were announcing a special on Fig Newtons." In his wise and empathetic first book, poet Stuart Dischell, through a variety of portraits and dramatic monologues, parses these singular voices from the sentence of human desire, illustrating how, as Michel de Montaigne wrote, "each man bears the entire form of man's estate."

Dischell teases secrets from everyday speech through scenes that begin with the ordinary and end in epiphany. Here is the would-be hero of "The Genius," who daydreams about pulling children from a fiery bus (or rescuing the Nobel committee): "…He feels he should have saved / His father from creditors and suicide / At fifty. 'Dad,' he says as he prizes / The old man's coffin, 'skeletons come alive.' " Just as the child's voice erupts in the poem's final lines, dependence and loss emerge from repression. Dischell knows how to put quirks of language to narrative use, as when the speaker in "The Bulletin Board" refers to his ex-girlfriend as "the other her." His accurate ear cherishes the voice of the storyteller while respecting the narratives people forge to frame their lives. When one of two buddies named Jerry appropriates the other's story, all hell breaks loose: "...at parties where neither is invited / Discussions break into fisticuffs and furniture / Gets smashed."

"Good Hope Road: America remains in your phrasing," Dischell writes in the collection's title poem, its homage to Whitman qualified by evidence that nowadays the open road also leads to the used car lot. More genial than cynical, Stuart Dischell's poems acknowledge the cramp of each individual's narrow place in the world. As the character in "Buddies" whose story is usurped tells his wife, "In the scheme of things / Our lives are a joke and we Jerrys are its comedians."

Joyce Peseroff coordinates Phone-a-Poem for Ploughshares. *Her most recent book of poetry,* A Dog in the Lifeboat, *was published by Carnegie Mellon University Press.*

TO PUT THE MOUTH TO *Poems by Judith Hall. Quill/William Morrow, $8.00 paper. Reviewed by Diann Blakely Shoaf.*

"To put the mouth to" is an old definition of *adorare,* and the phrase gives Judith Hall a memorable title while also providing a ground-bass for this musical and voluptuously intelligent first collection. "Love / Is difficult when not reduced to pulses / Sucking," she writes in one of the poems in "Fragments of an Eve: Scraps From Her Album"; in other work Hall examines the fine line between adoration and pornography. Women are worshipped for their beauty even as they are punished for it, assaulted through objectification, aesthetic and actual, "Cameos" implies. Taking the point even further, "A Wild Plum Is for Independence" suggests that masochism is woman's natural lot. Pleasure, for us, is usually derived from the same source as pain, and as a consequence, telling the difference between the two can be nearly impossible.

Yet while the ability to make distinctions, in life as in art, is one of the things that keeps us human, we are also human insofar as we are able to let difference and separation collapse in moments of pure pleasure: "No thought, nothing but circles of pink: / The mouth holds the body in place." And after reading *To Put the Mouth To,* surely no one would argue that such a function should be reserved for the mind or soul alone. The gorgeous textures of Hall's poems, woven as they are in equal parts of the sensuous and the spiritual, would have tempted, if not chastened, that avatar of asceticism, St. Augustine. "Lord keep us safe," a variation on his famous prayer, is a ubiquitous one in these dangerous times; still, Hall's poems echo his equally famous addendum: "but not yet."

Diann Blakely Shoaf's first book of poems, Hurricane Walk, *was published last year by BOA editions. She teaches at the Harpeth Hall School in Nashville.*

MY BODY TO YOU *Stories by Elizabeth Searle. Univ. of Iowa Press, $22.95. 1992 Iowa Short Fiction Award Winner, selected by James Salter. Reviewed by James Carroll.*

Elizabeth Searle has written these stories in fire. They are thirteen searing portraits of women or girls whose lives have taken them to the extreme of feeling—of loss, discovery, sensuality, self-hatred, passion, loneliness, and love.

The title of the collection offers a key to what distinguishes this work from other fiction. Each character Searle presents is so thoroughly rendered *in her body* that, to use a phrase from a separate, although not unconnected context, the word becomes flesh. Searle is not concerned with the mere appearance of her characters, or even the outer manifestations of inner states that conventional descriptions of gesture, physique, speech, or movement usually offer. This writer manages time and again to bring the reader into the very selves of her characters, obliterating the usual, Manichean division between the spiritual and the physical. "Our Bodies Ourselves" is the title of a famous feminist manifesto, but the phrase captures the spirit and meaning of these stories.

The title story, "My Body to You," concerns a young woman who, in her wish to love a man who cannot reciprocate, seeks in effect to leave her body by denying its needs. Because their physical love is impossible—he is gay—she will give him her self in the new state of a body freed from gravity, from the laws of the earth which keep her alone. In showing how the radical flight from the physical turns back on itself as the physical becomes all, this achingly beautiful story achieves in the end a pristine spirituality of desire.

In the story "What to Do in an Emergency," a recently divorced woman finds herself as a temp in a home for special-needs people. Searle gives us the home itself so vividly it becomes the body of the group living in it. "The uncovered bread dough had swollen. Bobbie Ann's stomach stirred at its sweet yeasty smell. It's flesh-colored curve nearly overflowed the bowl."

In "Number 8," a tour de force of restraint, the entirely unavailable world of an autistic boy becomes stunningly real not only for Ann, who becomes entranced with him, but for the reader, *through* her. Her profoundly physical perception throws her back to a key moment. "Dinosaurs have part of their brains in their tails. So which is the head? Ann had demanded. Wide awake for the first time ever in grade school science class, waving her hand at the teacher urgently." This moment of a girl's sudden—and solitary—awakening to the reversal of all she'd been taught captures the feel of what Elizabeth Searle has accomplished in this fine collection. She is waving her hand for all to see—a deft, writerly hand that works magic on the page. Searle's subject is the way women—the way all humans—press out from their bodies to connect, connect, connect, without ever thinking that is what we do, without knowing, really, which end is the head, and which the tail. Searle rivets and reveals, driving home in more than a dozen ways the hard truths—and the good news—that our brains are in both parts of us, that our bodies *are* the connection.

James Carroll is the author of eight novels, most recently Memorial Bridge. *His new novel,* Brothers, *will be published next winter. He teaches writing at Emerson College.*

PLOUGHSHARES POSTSCRIPTS

Miscellaneous Notes · Spring 1993

COMMONWEALTH AWARDS DeWitt Henry, Executive Director of *Ploughshares,* was among ten individuals and organizations selected for the 1993 Commonwealth Awards. Bestowed by the Massachusetts Cultural Council, the awards honor outstanding public service in the arts, humanities, and interpretive sciences in the state. Henry was recognized for his leadership of a small organization, "making *Ploughshares* an internationally renowned literary magazine that fosters diverse talent and new dialogues." As most of you know, Henry founded the journal in 1971 with Peter O'Malley, and he has guided *Ploughshares* through its tentative inception and many lean years to the level of prominence in the literary world that it enjoys today. Among the other winners were Henry Hampton and Stephen Jay Gould.

A NOTE TO OUR NEW SUBSCRIBERS Earlier this year, we conducted our first direct-mail campaign, which brought in over 1,200 new subscriptions. To all of you who took us up on our offer, welcome. We're grateful that you decided to join us, and we hope that you'll like reading *Ploughshares.* We'll do our best to merit your investment. Any time you have a problem with your subscription, please don't hesitate to call or write to us—third-class bulk mail can occasionally be unreliable. Thanks are also due to The Otto Group, a trio of magazine consultants, who helped us with the campaign: Lisa Newman and Bob and Kit Nylen.

WRITERS' HONORARIA In December 1992, the Lannan Foundation awarded *Ploughshares* with an $8,500 grant to increase the journal's cash honoraria to its writers and editors. The literary program at the Lannan Foundation, which is based in Los Angeles, was established in 1987 to stimulate the creation of high-quality, English-language literature and to increase public appreciation, understanding, and support for contemporary prose and poetry.

Previously, we paid $5 a page for poetry, with a minimum of $10 per poem, and $10 a page for prose, with a maximum of $50 for each author. With the Lannan Foundation grant, we will be able to offer, in 1993, $10 a page for both poetry and prose, with a $20 minimum and no maximum. Contributors will receive, as they did before, two complimentary copies and a one-year subscription. Of course, we realize that the honoraria are still woefully low as compensation for our writers' efforts, and this seems to be an industry-wide condition. In making a competitive analysis for our application to the foundation, we were surprised to discover that many reputable journals only reward their writers with copies, if that.

RANDOM FIRES A former Random House editor told us about a tour she took a few years ago of the publisher's huge warehouse and distribution center in Maryland. It was an impressive operation, she said, with "pickers," as they are called, efficiently carting around to collect books for orders. However, we were disheartened to hear what happened to the books after they had been remaindered and all attempts to sell them had been exhausted: the books were burned to heat the warehouse. We don't know if this is still a current practice. We hope not.

PRIZES Guest editor Louise Glück and series editor David Lehman have selected two *Ploughshares* works for inclusion in *The Best American Poetry 1993*: an untitled section of Killarney Clary's "Five Poems" and "Theory" by Paul Hoover, both of which appeared in the Winter 1991–92 issue, *Traces of Struggle and Desire*, edited by Carolyn Forché. By the way, Forché's anthology of works by poets who have endured conditions of extremity, *Against Forgetting: Twentieth Century Poetry of Witness*, has just been released by W.W. Norton.

COLOPHON In keeping with our new design, you'll be seeing new stationery from *Ploughshares* in the next few months. We're particularly pleased with the emblem that Sara Eisenman, who instituted the current journal design with the Winter 1992–93 issue, found for us in a book called *The Wood Engravings of Robert Gibbings.* Gibbings was a book artist and illustrator and the publisher of the Golden Cockerel Press. Thanks go to Patience Empson, Gibbings's literary executor, for giving us permission to adopt the 1923 engraving to symbolize the spirit of *Ploughshares.* Redesigning the journal, everyone agrees, is the smartest thing we've ever done. We're continually trying to justify and exceed our reputation as one of the finest literary magazines in the country. We should *look* like one of the best as well.

"Colophon" is usually defined today as a statement about a book's production, rather than as a trade emblem. Thus, we have an excuse to talk about our in-house production process, which people ask about more and more frequently. Most of our prose contributors are able to give us diskettes of their work, which we transfer and convert to Microsoft Word on one of our three IBM clones. Although a scanner is accessible to us on the Emerson campus, we prefer to type in all the poetry, which allows us to be more sensitive to line- and spacebreaks. We print out initial manuscript proofs on an HP LaserJet III, make copy edits and corrections, then transfer everything to our Mac IIci, importing the Word files into our typesetting program, QuarkXPress 3.1. We use the Adobe Minion type family throughout the issue. Galleys are printed on the HP, and after the final corrections are made by the authors and staff, we send diskettes of PostScript files to our printer, Edwards Brothers, who outputs directly to negatives and then sheetfeeds the issue on Glatfelter natural paper. The same basic composition process holds true for the color separations of our covers, which are done by Colortronix. Bringing all of this in-house has been cost-efficient and surprisingly easy, and has transformed our production values. (The same cannot be said about our decision to continue fulfilling all subscription orders ourselves; the volume is getting out of hand, but that's a problem we will gladly live with.) It's a different world. Five years ago, we did not have a single computer in our office.

—Don Lee

MFA

Writing Program
at Vermont College

Intensive 11-Day residencies
July on the Vermont campus; January in Florida.
Workshops, classes, readings, conferences, followed
by **Non-Resident 6-Month Writing Projects** in
poetry and fiction individually designed during residency.
In-depth criticism of manuscripts. Sustained dialogue with faculty.

Post-graduate Writing Semester
for those who have already finished a graduate degree
with a concentration in creative writing.

Vermont College admits students
regardless of race, creed, sex or ethnic origin.

Scholarships and financial aid available.

Low-residency B.A. and M.A. programs also available.

Faculty

Tony Ardizzone	Phyllis Barber
Francois Camoin	Mark Cox
Deborah Digges	Mark Doty
Jonathan Holden	Lynda Hull
Richard Jackson	Sydney Lea
Diane Lefer	Ellen Lesser
Susan Mitchell	Jack Myers
Sena Jeter Naslund	Christopher Noel
Pamela Painter	David Rivard
Gladys Swan	Sharon Sheehe Stark
Leslie Ullman	Belle Waring
Roger Weingarten	W.D. Wetherell
David Wojahn	

Visiting Writers include:

Julia Alvarez	Linda Bierds
Maureen McCoy	Bruce Weigl

For more information:
Roger Weingarten, MFA Writing Program, Box 889,
Vermont College of Norwich University, Montpelier, VT 05602
802–828–8840

Celebrating 25 Years of the Pitt Poetry Series!

The Pittsburgh Book of Contemporary American Poetry

Ed Ochester and Peter Oresick, Editors

This anthology commemorates the twenty-fifth anniversary of the Pitt Poetry Series (1968–1993), providing generous selections—about three hundred lines of verse—of the forty-five poets currently in print in the series, as well as a full-page photograph of each.

The Pittsburgh Book of Contemporary American Poetry is an ideal and inexpensive anthology for classroom use in literature and creative writing courses, and the best available general introduction to contemporary American poetry for the general reader.

Poets Included

Claribel Alegría, Debra Allbery, Maggie Anderson, Robin Becker, Siv Cedering, Lorna Dee Cervantes, Nancy Vieria Couto, Kate Daniels, Toi Derricotte, Sharon Doubiago, Stuart Dybek, Jane Flanders, Gary Gildner, Elton Glaser, David Huddle, Lawrence Joseph, Julia Kasdorf, Etheridge Knight, Bill Knott, Ted Kooser, Larry Levis, Irene McKinney, Peter Meinke, Carol Muske, Leonard Nathan, Sharon Olds, Alicia Suskin Ostriker, Greg Pape, Kathleen Peirce, David Rivard, Liz Rosenberg, Maxine Scates, Richard Shelton, Betsy Sholl, Peggy Shumaker, Jeffrey Skinner, Gary Soto, Leslie Ullman, Constance Urdang, Ronald Wallace, Belle Waring, Michael S. Weaver, Robley Wilson, David Wojahn, Paul Zimmer.

Paper $15.95

Available at bookstores, or

University of Pittsburgh Press

C/O CUP SERVICES, BOX 6525, ITHACA, NY 14851   800-666-2211

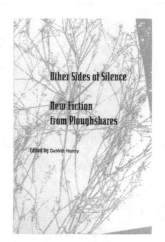

BENNINGTON
WRITING
WORKSHOPS

JULY 4 - JULY 17 AND
JULY 18 - JULY 31 1993

16TH YEAR

For more information, contact:
Liam Rector, Director
Bennington Writing Workshops
Bennington College, Box PL
Bennington, Vermont 05201
802-442-5401, ext. 320

ACADEMIC CREDIT AVAILABLE

A member of *Writers' Conferences & Festivals* wc&f

FACULTY:
Sven Birkerts
Stephen Dobyns
Percival Everett
Dana Gioia
Barry Hannah
Elinor Lipman
Bret Lott
Jill McCorkle
Jane Miller
Liam Rector
Roxana Robinson
Bob Shacochis

READERS:
Frank Bidart
Lucie Brock-Broido
Nicholas Delbanco
Donald Hall
John Irving
Jane Kenyon
Jamaica Kincaid
David Lehman
Ed Ochester
Stephen Sandy
Louis Simpson

EDITORS & PUBLISHERS:
Jonathan Galassi
Carol Houck Smith
and others

HEAVEN

COLLECTED POEMS
1 9 5 6 – 1 9 9 0

A L   Y O U N G

"The power of Young's poetry comes from his refusal to allow himself to in any way be segregated from the world. He is bold, he is blunt, but above all he is full of affection of the past and hope for the future."
Louis L. Martz, *Yale Review*

"Both the good feeling and the good poetry result from Al Young's poetic vantage point. He seems to be a man happy with his present, and on good speaking terms with his past."
Rolling Stone

"The pace of these poems is fast, jazzy, propelling the reader along with supple, often conversational rhythms, lively description and rushes of feeling."
Library Journal

"Al Young has a rare gift among contemporary poets: eloquence. It is rare because it requires having a bit of wisdom and the feel for what language can do."
Charles Simic, Pulitzer Prize-winning poet

360pp., 5¼×8¼
ISBN 0-88739-068-4 Cloth 24.95
ISBN 0-88739-069-2 Paper 17.95

CREATIVE ARTS BOOK COMPANY
833 BANCROFT WAY • BERKELEY, CALIFORNIA 94710
FAX: 1-510-848-4844 • PHONE 1-800-848-7789

the modern writer as witness

Eat, Drink &
Be Literary.

HARVARD BOOK STORE
CAFE

Breakfast through Late Dinner
190 Newbury Street at Exeter, Boston • 536-0095

Ploughshares Submission Policies

Ploughshares is published three times a year: one fiction issue and two mixed issues of poetry and fiction. Each is guest-edited by a different writer, and often he or she will be interested in specific themes or aesthetics. Before you submit, you should check if we are seeking something in particular and query for deadlines. You may either send a business-sized, self-addressed, stamped envelope and ask for detailed writer's guidelines, or call the *Ploughshares* answering machine at night, after 8 p.m., Eastern Time, for a recorded announcement: (617) 578-8753. Please do not call before 8 p.m., even on weekends. Postmark submissions to *Ploughshares,* Emerson College, 100 Beacon St., Boston, MA 02116-1596, between August 1 and April 1 (returned unread during the summer). This is a new schedule; we will honor the old deadline of April 30 in 1993 only. Overall, we look for submissions of serious literary value. For poetry, limit of 3–5 poems. Individually typed either single- or double-spaced on one side of the page. (Phone-a-Poem is by invitation only.) For prose, one story, novel excerpt, memoir, or personal essay. No criticism or book reviews. Thirty-page maximum. Typed double-spaced on one side of the page. Mail poetry and prose separately. Only one submission of poetry and/or prose at a time. Do not submit separately for different issues/editors, and do not send another manuscript until you hear about the first. Additional submissions will be returned unread. All submissions are first screened at our office; staff editors determine for which issue/editor a work is most appropriate, and if an issue closes, the work is considered for the next one(s). Never send directly to a guest editor; the manuscript will be discarded unread. Please write your full name and address on the outside envelope and address it to either Poetry, Fiction, or Nonfiction Editor. All manuscripts and correspondence regarding submissions should be accompanied by a self-addressed, stamped envelope for reply or return of the manuscript, or we will not respond. We cannot accommodate revisions, changes of return address, or forgotten S.A.S.E.'s after the fact. Expect three to five months for a decision. Simultaneous submissions are permitted. We cannot be responsible for loss, delay, or damage.

PLOUGHSHARES
INTERNATIONAL WRITING SEMINAR

CASTLE WELL, THE NETHERLANDS
EMERSON COLLEGE EUROPEAN CENTER

AUGUST 15-27, 1993
FOURTH ANNUAL SEMINAR
CO-DIRECTORS: JAMES CARROLL AND ROBIE MACAULEY

An intensive fiction writing workshop held in a Renaissance castle in the placid Dutch countryside. Twenty to thirty selected writers work with a distinguished faculty and fellow seminar members from many countries. Some participants are short story writers, some are novelists; some are published writers, some are in early stages of promising careers. All work in English. Team-taught morning workshops, afternoon writing and conference sessions, evening readings and roundtables. Emphasis on individual instruction. Four academic credits. All in a beautiful setting in the heart of the New Europe. CO-DIRECTORS: James Carroll and Robie Macauley. FACULTY: Pamela Painter, Alexandra Marshall, Thomas E. Kennedy, and a rotation of guest speakers.

FOR APPLICATION INFORMATION, CONTACT:
David Griffin · Division of Continuing Education
Emerson College · 100 Beacon St. · Boston, MA 02116
TEL (617) 578-8615 · FAX (617) 578-8618